BLESS THE DYING

BLESS THE DYING

SANDRA BRETTING

FIVE STAR
A part of Gale, Cengage Learning

GALE
CENGAGE Learning·

Farmington Hills, Mich • San Francisco • New York • Waterville, Maine
Meriden, Conn • Mason, Ohio • Chicago

Copyright © 2014 by Sandra Bretting.
Five Star™ Publishing, a part of Gale, Cengage Learning.

LIBRARY OF CONGRESS CATALOGING-IN-PUBLICATION DATA

Bretting, Sandra.
  Bless the dying / Sandra Bretting. First edition.
    pages cm
    ISBN 978-1-4328-2879-0 (hardcover) — ISBN 1-4328-2879-7
(hardcover)
    1. Police—Crimes against—Fiction. 2. Poisoning—Fiction. 3.
Criminal investigation—Fiction. I. Title.
  PS3602.R4586B54 2014
  813/. 6—23   2014011936

First Edition. First Printing: August 2014
Find us on Facebook– https://www.facebook.com/FiveStarCengage
Visit our website– http://www.gale.cengage.com/fivestar/
Contact Five Star™ Publishing at FiveStar@cengage.com

Printed in the United States of America
1 2 3 4 5 6 7 18 17 16 15 14

For my parents, Jerry and Cornelia Lanting—who gave me the gift of good books and a light to read them by.

ACKNOWLEDGMENTS

Once a book is written there are so many people to thank and not enough space to do so. First of all, this book and my writing career wouldn't be possible without the support of my husband, Roger, who loves me despite my ongoing affair with the written word. I'd also like to thank my daughters—Brooke and Dana—for making me laugh even when the world doesn't seem particularly funny.

For bringing my very first novel to light, thank you so much to Tiffany Schofield and Deni Dietz of Five Star Publishing. And for always believing in my work, thanks go out to my writing partner of more than a decade, Susan Breeden.

For helping me learn about the art and the business of writing, a big thank you to members of the Writers' League of Texas. The camaraderie of other writers and the wealth of information provided by the League have proven invaluable. My sincere gratitude also to members of the Heart of Texas Chapter of Sisters in Crime. It was they who first encouraged me by choosing my work for the Barbara Burnett Smith Aspiring Writers Program, for which I'll always be grateful.

For passages in this book involving medicine and medical diagnoses, I received invaluable advice from several doctors, pharmacists, and nurses. One of them in particular—Melody Bolin, RN—never tired of my many emails and beginner's questions. The accuracies in this book belong to those talented professionals, while any mistakes are mine.

Acknowledgments

Finally, I'd like to offer my heartfelt thanks to you, the reader. Without people who love and appreciate the written word, writers would be unnecessary. Thank you for making books necessary.

PROLOGUE

*Give Thy angels and saints charge over those who
    sleep.*
*Rest the weary ones, bless the dying ones, soothe the
    suffering ones.*

—From a Catholic evening prayer by Saint Augustine

CHAPTER 1

By the time the telephone message arrived, another Monday morning staff briefing at St. James Medical Center had come and gone. The pale blue note lay on top of a dozen others, all waiting for Rhetta Day when she returned to her office in the public relations department.

Amazing how quickly the pages multiplied. Just beyond her cluttered desk, a plump midmorning sun beckoned through the window, perched on top of the patient care tower as if gathering strength for its journey across the Southern California sky. Below the roofline, a blurry figure moved back and forth, back and forth, inside one of the patient's rooms.

She plucked up the first telephone message and winced, as if bitten by the words. The note said something about an accident with Nick Tahari and the hospital's seventh floor, which, everyone knew, was reserved for the sickest patients of all. Why, even the doctors joked that the unit, found at the very top of the hospital, was placed there because it was closest to God.

"What's wrong?" Her assistant, Wanda LaPorte, hovered in the doorway.

"They brought in someone I know. To the seventh floor."

"Intensive care? What happened?" Quickly, Wanda bustled in and perched on a corner of the desk in a whorl of polyester.

"I don't know." The ICU usually meant a heart attack or stroke, car crash or aneurysm, something that happened to other people, older people, one step short of death. Something

11

that couldn't be handled several floors below. ICU was neon stickers on every other door—"Infectious Disease. No admittance!"—and nurses who whispered urgently back and forth. "Can you hold my calls?"

"Sure, boss." But Wanda didn't move. She lingered, obviously trolling for more information she could dangle over the other assistants during lunch.

"Thanks. And please shut my door."

With that, Wanda grudgingly relinquished her perch and left, softly shutting the door behind her.

The last place Rhetta wanted to visit was the seventh floor. Ever since Nick became a cop, she dreaded what could happen. His friends all thought he would put in for desk duty, or that's what they'd hoped would happen, but he insisted on patrolling South Central Los Angeles, at night, where even the trash haulers refused to pick up garbage bins before ten o'clock in the morning. No one would breathe easier until the night had fully passed and the Locos and Primos, the Swags and the Playboys, were all safely asleep in graffitied apartment buildings that sat hard up on the Golden State Freeway.

Oh, Nick. How could he do this? Even though it had been weeks since she last saw him, a pitcher of beer in one hand and a dripping mug in the other, it seemed like a moment ago.

She dropped the telephone message and journeyed from her office to a hospital elevator that waited at the end of the hall. When she reached the seventh floor, the door whooshed open to reveal a woman wearing maroon surgical scrubs. Nick's wife, Beryl, worked as a coronary care nurse and she knew the hospital better than anyone.

"Beryl! Where is he?"

"Room seven-fifteen."

Together they swept through the waiting room and headed for room 715. They passed an old man first, who looked grief-stricken, hunched forward like that, but Beryl didn't seem to notice. After five years of working as a coronary care nurse, she didn't seem bothered by the sight of grieving people, the smell of ammonia, or the frigid slap of air conditioning.

"Was it a gunshot?" Rhetta searched for a clue on her friend's face—maybe in her eyes—for what awaited her once they reached Nick's room.

"No. Nothing like that. He was supposed to go in for a test this morning, so he took some medicine last night. It wasn't supposed to be a big deal. But something went wrong." When she glanced Rhetta's way, it was as if someone had thrown a switch and the worried wife gave way to the highly trained professional. "It's called acute respiratory distress. They couldn't handle it at the local community hospital, so they brought him here."

Rhetta cocked her head. "A test?"

"Thyroid scan. He had an allergic reaction to the tracer. Come on."

She followed Beryl into the room. Nick had been folded into an envelope of starched white cotton, and two clear tubes ran from his nose to a plastic box dotted with red and black knobs that were turned every which way. She desperately wanted to wrench the tubes out.

"Is he conscious?"

"He's pretty drugged up." Gently, Beryl took Nick's wrist, turned it over, and lovingly placed two of her fingers crosswise against his skin, like a woman applying perfume there. She seemed to be timing his pulse against her watch.

As she waited, Rhetta debated whether to sit on the bed or stand perched over his body, so she compromised by leaning halfway and pressing her elbows against the chilled steel rail. "Hi, Nick. I came to see how you are."

His eyelids fluttered before fully opening. He stared at her, as

13

if he was trying to read her lips, and his own lips were parched. After a moment, he reached for a pen and a pad of yellow sticky notes someone had laid on the bed, and weakly scrawled something onto the pad. *I'm scared*, he scribbled.

For an instant her heart stilled. This was the man who was so excited to finally fire his police rifle that he'd bought a round of drinks at their favorite bar, The Corner Pocket, to celebrate. Nick had jumped up on the bar, wearing an eyepatch, and proceeded to tell them all about how he had been ambushed by a street gang. Seems the gang had lured him to an abandoned house in South Central with a nine-twenty-one—report of a prowler—but when he got there, gunfire rained down. Thankfully, the gangsters were terrible shots, and all he had to show for it was a bullet's skid mark across his forehead. This man, lying in front of her now, breathing through plastic, was one of the few officers who dared patrol the worst streets of Los Angeles at two o'clock in the morning, when they were peopled with crack addicts, gangbangers, and homeless runaways. How could he be scared? "C'mon, Nick. You'll be out of here in no time."

He nudged the pad back 'round again and lifted the pen once more. *Scared as hell*, he wrote.

She straightened after reading the words. "What's going on, Beryl?"

"Someone messed up the test. His body shut down and he couldn't breathe. It was horrible. So now he's on oxygen to stabilize his pulse and his heart."

Rhetta drew closer to Nick's side after hearing that. At the foot of his bed, peeking out from under the crisp white sheet, was a pair of high-top tennis shoes with the toes pointed straight in the air. They made Nick look like Gulliver tied to his resting place, huge feet askew, as if he was waiting for a Lilliputian to rescue him.

"Foot drop," Beryl said, watching her. She had once again switched into an official-sounding nurse's voice. "They'll help keep his feet up."

Rhetta didn't know whether to laugh or to cry. If Nick was able, he probably would have laughed and made a joke about always being ready for a quick game of one-on-one basketball. Ever since their college days, Nick had a hard time taking anything seriously, except for his beloved basketball.

"Look, can you call some of our friends and let them know?" Beryl finally asked. "Tell them not to visit, though. Nick would hate for them to see him like this. His partner already knows, and I told him it's okay to come up here. Help me out on this one, will you?"

As if she had to ask. "Of course. Just let me know what you need. Are they treating you okay?"

"Yeah, they've been great. He's got some of the best docs on staff. He's even got a buddy here. Some guy from high school named Eamon McAllister." Tenderly, she lifted Nick's wrist once more as he dozed.

"I hate to do this, Beryl, but I've got to get back to work. If there's anything I can do, anything at all, please let me know." She turned toward Nick a final time to study his face, and it dawned on her then that she was waiting for him to wake up with a big yawn, as if he were only rising from a catnap. But his face was far more shiny than normal, and a rivulet of sweat had begun to line his upper lip. What she wanted to do—what she would have done if Beryl wasn't standing by her side—was to dip lower and kiss Nick's damp cheek. Somehow, she would let him know that everything was going to be all right, and he and his high-top tennis shoes soon would walk out of these catacombs. Only she doubted Beryl would understand that. Their past was just that—in the past. For now all she could manage was a weak smile before slipping away from his bedside.

CHAPTER 2

Licorice. No one had told him the medicine would taste like licorice. The stuff had even smelled like a licorice stick you get at the movies, but only if they're out of the good stuff and it's a crummy chick flick and there's nothing to do but eat.

Nick's head lolled against the hospital pillow now. The funny thing was, when the tech gave him the medicine to take home, it was in a plastic cup with Braille ridges. Reminded him of the one he had to pee into at the police academy for the physical exam. By that time he was more than halfway through his police department tests—there were eight, count them, eight of them altogether—so he gladly took a piss and gave the clerk the cup back, knowing full well he was clean. He hadn't smoked a joint since college, since that night Rhetta gave him the "just friends" speech, right after he'd whupped her ass at speed quarters and asked her to come back with him to his dorm room. When she said no, he decided it was either go home alone and get stoned, or trash the place.

He hated licorice. He'd only agreed to take the thyroid test so they'd all stop bugging him. His partner, his wife; hell, even his dog would probably bug him if he could. All those big words—radioactive uptake, thyroxine—they meant zero to him, but they seemed to make everyone else feel like a big shot, so he said fine, all right already, he'd go in and take the scan. As long as someone else took care of the details.

The starched pillow scratched against his cheek now. After he

16

took the medicine, he had tried to watch his favorite cable show—the one with the pudgy cartoon characters in rainbow colors—but it was too late for that. He liked the basic colors, the hokey songs, the silly dances, the way they all got along. The show mesmerized him. It sometimes lulled him back to sleep, and those were the best times, because he would dream about the colorful characters and daisies that talked and sugary-white clouds. Anything to take his mind off the falling-down crack houses, the bloody bar brawls, the meth-heads who had better weapons than he did, the wife beaters with their swaggers. Anything to soften the edges, to give him some peace, even if it was only for half an hour, and then he'd have to get up again anyway and do the whole thing over.

Beryl was the only one who knew his little cartoon secret, and that was okay. He could trust his wife, bossy or not; he could trust her with his life. She would have made a great cop, because she was as dependable as your next breath. After they'd had sex on their first date—she seemed to want it more than him, and who wouldn't dig that?—he'd felt obliged to call her. One thing led to another until he said, sure, why not, I'll marry you. Go pick out a ring you like. They'd been together five peaceful, predictable, cartoon-filled years.

He didn't notice anything was wrong last night, until he felt his throat tighten, like it was shrinking, somehow, little by little. Like it was forcing air up, not down, not where it belonged. He had gulped once or twice and looked at his dog, who had just sat there and cocked his head, like there was a big furry question mark over it.

When he inhaled again, something whistled in his throat. Like a wheeze, that came out of nowhere and went into his sinuses, then slowly worked its way down his windpipe. He could hear Beryl call his name, felt someone shake his shoulder, but he couldn't respond.

17

Now, lying there in the hospital bed, desperately trying to breathe in, breathe out, breathe in, breathe out, he thought he heard a dog whimper. *Don't worry, boy. I'll be back before you know it. Don't you worry.*

I can't believe people eat this stuff. By lunchtime, Rhetta was in the bowels of the main hospital tower, turning over a clump of iceberg lettuce in the cafeteria's salad bar. But the lettuce leaf looked wilted, yellow, forlorn in the fake wood-grain bowl. The salad bar was a new addition to the hospital's cafeteria; a halfhearted attempt to offer something healthy for lunch instead of the usual French fries and sloppy joes. Most times people avoided the salads altogether, and made a beeline for the grill and a sloppy pile of onion rings.

She turned over the limp leaves, picking and choosing between an anemic baby carrot and a lopsided tomato, before finally giving up. She joined the shortest line, which arced toward the cash register. The place was crowded again—there wasn't an empty booth in sight—just clusters of employees hunched over their lunch trays, which was the price she paid for being so punctual and eating at twelve o'clock on the dot.

Nothing to do but watch and wait, lockstep to the register, pop the tomato into her mouth, and mash seeds against her tongue. The man in front of her wore surgical scrubs, which meant he was probably a tech or a resident, since none of the doctors she knew was humble enough to eat in the employee cafeteria. She watched the stranger bounce on the balls of his feet, a dark curl bobbing in time, so maybe he was a medical resident, after all, since they were always in a hurry.

The man's curl kept bouncing, even after he stopped. Bored, she reached for a baby carrot on her plate, which pushed her tray smack-dab into the one ahead of it, spilling some of her drink onto the floor. That made the stranger turn—he had a chiseled face topped by tousled brown hair—so she quickly licked some ranch dressing from her palm, plunged her fist into her blazer pocket, and rummaged around for change, pretending not to notice him.

Finally, the stranger paid for his meal, and grabbed his tray to leave. When he turned, she instinctively peeked at a rectangular nametag pinned to his chest. *Eamon McAllister, M.D.*

Wasn't that the name of the doctor from Nick's high school, the one Beryl had told her about?

"Dr. McAllister?" She had to speak up, what with the overhead music and all, and it made the question sound more like an accusation than anything else.

"Yes?"

"I know a patient of yours, I think." Quickly, she fished out two crumpled dollar bills and handed them across the conveyor belt to the cashier, who had perked up at the exchange. "Nick Tahari. Admitted this morning?"

"Yes, of course." He paused then, as if trying to make up his mind about something. Whatever it was, he seemed to come to a decision. "Are you eating alone?"

She blinked. He was extremely good-looking, but he was also a complete stranger. She was about to tell him that when a tone sounded from somewhere around the man's waist. Frowning, the stranger punched at a beeper that was clipped to his scrubs.

"I'm sorry. It's an emergency. Some other time?"

"No problem." Her smile slipped as she watched him walk away, the boyish curl keeping time with his steps. Out of all the people she could have run into, what were the odds she'd meet up with a friend of Nick's? Their two worlds were colliding once again, after spending so much time apart. After building separate lives for the past five years, minute by minute and day by day.

She scanned the crowded lunchroom, which was raucous

with the sound of laughter and conversation. It looked like she would have to eat lunch alone, surrounded by the company of strangers . . . again.

Wanda wasn't at her post when Rhetta returned to the PR office after lunch. She never did finish the salad, and had to settle for two smashed crackers instead. Her secretary was no doubt on one of her infamous "errands," which meant Wanda had slipped away, unnoticed, with a few interoffice envelopes tucked under her arm for good measure.

By now, her assistant could be anywhere in the medical center—maybe chatting with a radiology receptionist, conniving with a janitor, or reclining against the pharmacy counter in pediatrics. Wherever she was, Wanda was much too social to be stuck in her own department, minding the lot of them.

Come to think of it, maybe Wanda would know what to make of Nick's illness. Aside from what Beryl had said, which wasn't much, she didn't understand why Nick was lying upstairs in ICU, as one machine breathed for him while another monitored his heartbeat. Why was he so weak that even rotating a sticky note had taken all of his strength? The only things she knew had come from Beryl, and she didn't want to pester her with more questions.

She reached across Wanda's desk for a telephone, and dialed the secretary's cell number. Wherever Wanda was in the hospital, she couldn't have found it too interesting because she picked up on the second ring. "Where are you, Wanda?" An intercom crackled loudly in the background.

"First floor, lobby. What's up?"

She could imagine Wanda squinting at the glowing cell phone, wondering why Rhetta would track her down, when she had never bothered to before. "I need some help. Are you next to the info desk?"

The information desk at St. James sat squarely in the center of the lobby. Rounded into a half-moon, it was home to two PBX consoles with matching computer screens. Everyone gathered around it—visitors, doctors, vendors, volunteers. A few years before, when the hospital didn't even have fiber optic buttons or flat panel screens, Wanda had been the receptionist there.

She must have noticed Rhetta's awestruck face on first seeing the buzzers and contraptions, because she'd offered to give her a tour. She told her then that up until a few years ago, she could say anything she wanted to people who called, as loudly as she wanted, without a second thought. She could tell someone that, yes, a new mother was doing very well, but her baby didn't look so hot. Or, she would tell a caller that a certain pastor's recovery was coming along fine, thank you, now that he had finally wised up and started taking his medicine. She could announce almost anything to the people standing around the desk, and no one would ever reprimand her.

But then the tide turned. Patient privacy became key. Three little letters governed what Wanda could, and couldn't, say after that: ADT. The letters stood for admission, discharge, and transfer, but she said they might as well have stood for "a damn thing," because that's what she couldn't say, she had complained.

Of course, it was all part of the Health Insurance Portability and Accountability Act, but Rhetta wasn't about to remind Wanda of that. The rule was supposed to keep nosy people from checking in on their pastors or, worse yet, long-lost relatives from pestering new mothers with sick babies. It had gotten so bad, Wanda had insisted, she couldn't even say where a patient had been sent. As if they would let a person wander out the front door, fresh from the operating room, with a suitcase in one hand and an IV pole in the other, for heaven's sake.

Rhetta knew she was asking for trouble now, but she had to risk it. "Look, Wanda, I need you to check on a patient in the computer."

"I don't know, Rhetta."

"C'mon. This is important." Her secretary had buddied up to half the hospital, and if she wanted to find out something about Nick, she could. A regular magician, Wanda could unearth anything . . . from what the chief executive officer had for breakfast to whether the head of human resources was still hitting on the accounting temp. Even what day Nick was due to be transferred out of the ICU. "Please, Wanda."

There were mumbles in the background, the receiver stifled by Wanda's palm, no doubt, and after a moment, she returned. "Okay, I'll do it. But it'll cost you."

Great . . . now they were bartering for patient information, in broad daylight, with the world walking right by the information desk, no less. "Depends. What do you want?"

"Candy. Something good. None of that cheap stuff."

"Done." She patted the pocket of her blazer, where a few quarters rubbed the lining. "The patient's name is Nick Tahari. He was admitted this morning to ICU."

"Your friend, right? The cop?"

"Yeah. I need to know if he's stabilized. Anything at all."

Wanda fell silent, and the tap of a computer key sounded in the background. Finally, she spoke up again. "Sorry, but his info's been restricted. There's some kind of note here. It says 'access denied.' " The typing had stopped, as well as whispers in the background.

"What does that mean?"

"It means someone put the kibosh on his records. Sorry about that."

"But don't you remember the access code?" She was biting into her words now. It wasn't Wanda's fault, she knew that, but

Wanda was the messenger here, after all. If there was one thing she despised it was being told no, and today wasn't any different.

"Yeah, I remember the code for general stuff. But if information's been restricted, there's nothing I can do."

How strange. Someone had placed Nick's information off-limits. If anyone called—didn't matter if it was a concerned friend, or a specialist at another hospital, or even his lieutenant back at the police station—he wouldn't show up as a patient. Someone had made sure of that.

"By the way, Rhetta, you still have to pay up. They have the fancy chocolates in the gift shop."

"What? Oh, yeah." Why would someone restrict the information? It didn't make sense, unless something else was going on. An idea started to form, but she quickly dismissed it. "I'll get you the candy as soon as I can."

Slowly, Rhetta hung up the telephone. If anyone knew how to work the system at St. James, it was Wanda. If she couldn't tell her how long Nick would remain in the intensive care unit, if she couldn't give her the slightest hint about what had brought him to this point, then she would have to go straight to the source.

Much as she hated to bother Beryl, she would never be able to concentrate until she understood Nick's diagnosis. Without a word, she left the office and began to walk down the executive corridor, her footfalls softened by plush carpet.

Elegant taupe walls passed by in a blur. The muted color provided a fitting backdrop for the expensive oil paintings hanging there. The executive's corridor was quiet, which was unusual for a Monday afternoon, because normally people would hustle along clutching status reports, census charts, and who knew what else, as they scurried from one meeting to the next. No one ever strolled in the executive offices, they rushed. As if the hospital couldn't survive one . . . second . . . longer . . . until they reached their destinations.

But not today. Today, the hall stood empty, and recessed lights cast perfect, undisturbed ovals on the Berber carpet. If the hospital had multiple personalities—which it did—the executive suite would be a rich uncle in his brocade vest smoking a fat cigar. Patients never knew of this other, rarified world, because they were never allowed to enter it, which seemed to suit the executives just fine.

But the lobby . . . that was her portal to the normal world. She arrived there as if propelled through a hermetically sealed tube, and found herself in the midst of crying babies, scampering toddlers, graying hospital volunteers, and a burly construction worker or two in blue jeans. Here, people went about their business in the open, with no thought about who might be watching them or whether they looked important enough. She could finally breathe again. She worked her way through the throng, to the elevator, and rode it to the fifth floor. When the doors slid open, she beheld a cluttered nurses' station.

The coronary care unit was one of the busiest units in the whole hospital. Doctors, nurses, technicians, clerks, dieticians, therapists—everyone buzzed around the patients here. What with the minute-by-minute monitoring, the lives that hung in the balance, the heart surgeons and respiratory technicians stopping by at all hours of the day and night, there was always someone coming and going. A skinny nurse manned the station, and she barely glanced up as Rhetta approached her. "Can I help you?"

"I'd like to speak with Beryl Tahari." The nurse sighed, as if Rhetta had asked her to pull a double shift on her day off. "Please," she added.

"Just a minute. Tahari's around here somewhere."

Rhetta pondered the floor as the nurse fluttered her hands

over the chaotic desk, then thrust her fist into a pile of patient charts and withdrew a microphone. Before she could announce Beryl's name, though, another nurse sidled up and whispered something to her. They both eyed Rhetta, and the skinny nurse lowered the microphone. "We have a code blue. You'll have to step aside."

Code blues meant a medical emergency, which would summon a train of doctors, nurses, orderlies, and whoever else was handy. The staff only used it when a patient was in shock, and Rhetta had once seen an entire hall of people throw themselves against the walls to make room for a stretcher after hearing those two, innocuous words.

She ducked through a door to get out of the way. The room she stood in was bright with afternoon sun, and it smelled of rubbing alcohol and scorched cotton. She had entered a patient's room, or rather a room for two patients, because a thin blue curtain bisected the space. Boxy monitors the color of sand stood against the wall, and a pair of television sets had been riveted to the roof with heavy screws. Unlike the maternity unit downstairs, with its dancing teddy bears and joyful colors, here everything was functional and clean and sparse.

The blue curtain had been drawn the length of the room. The first bed was empty, but low voices could be heard behind the drape. Something rippled it from the other side—an elbow, perhaps—as things were repositioned there. When that something poked extra hard against the curtain, a voice whimpered.

"It's okay," a softer voice responded. Rhetta recognized the speaker immediately.

"Beryl?" The curtain drew back, maneuvered by Beryl, who had taken control of that section of the room. She obviously was conducting a test of some kind, for she had taken up a small amount of blood from the patient into a plastic syringe. The person lay quietly on the bed now and held one withered

25

arm in the air.

"Hi, Rhetta." Beryl smiled as she gently lowered the patient's arm. "I was just getting a sample." The patient, with hair as white as the starched pillow, turned back to the window.

"Doesn't that hurt?" Rhetta took a step closer.

"Unfortunately, yes. But it's got to be done." Tenderly, Beryl placed the patient's arm under the sheet, and slid the syringe into her pocket. "We'll try again later." She tilted her head, and stepped around the bed. "Did you need something?"

"Yes. No. I don't know." Beryl seemed so efficient; a true professional. "I was going to ask you about Nick."

"I don't know what to tell you," Beryl said, as she drew the curtain closed. "They don't have a real diagnosis yet."

"But it must be pulmonary, right? I saw a ventilator."

She nodded. "Yes, it's pulmonary. That much we know. I got him here as quick as I could."

"I'm sure you did. Did anyone else know about Nick's test?"

"Well, his partner, of course." Beryl glanced back at the patient, but all was quiet on the other side of the curtain. She seemed to want to say more, but before she could speak again, static from the paging system sounded overhead.

"Code blue. Code blue."

Beryl turned toward the door. "I've gotta go." Briskly, efficiently, she straightened her uniform. "His police partner knows everything. I'd check with him if I were you." She said the last few words over her shoulder, as she walked through the double-wide door.

CHAPTER 3

As Nick lay on a strange hospital bed, he felt pain, searing pain, in his abdomen. He jammed his knuckles there. He heard a man's voice—who was he and why was he yelling?—but he couldn't answer him; it would take too much energy. So he lay there, inert, on the intractable bed, and his body began to relax. His brain fired information back and forth, back and forth, reaching deeper into the files of his memory. The memories whizzed him past last night to more than five years earlier: to the night he first met Rhetta Day.

How could he forget? It was during Hell Week at the fraternity, sometime in September. Out of the blue, the frat members had decided to throw a makeshift luau, complete with phony palm trees and travel posters stuck to the walls. The place looked almost decent by the time they were through with it, considering it wasn't really a house at all, but a duplex one of the dads had bought for them out of pity. Nick had hung out on the balcony most of the time, next to the keg, of course. A few girls showed up early, but they weren't particularly fun to talk to, so he stood with his buddies and tried not to think about much at all.

After an hour or so, he remembered he got tired of bullshitting and worked his way to the back of the place. Halfway there, a roar erupted from a bathroom in the rear, so he laid his beer on a stereo speaker and wandered over to the sound.

Hell, but it was loud. He didn't know how many people could

fit into one bathroom, but there were so many people in *this* bathroom, the walls were shaking. The door was closed, so he threw it open and there was a crowd hovering around an old bathtub that no one had ever gotten around to cleaning, and no one ever used. Well, not as a bathtub, anyway.

It looked like they were using it for a dunk tank tonight, because he could see a blond head jerk up and down in the bathtub. Some poor guy was getting dunked in the alcohol. Probably one of his pledge brothers. He took a step closer, and shoved his elbow between two of the actives until finally they let him through. Yeah, it was a pledge all right, and the kid was spitting up purple, the color of fruit punch mixed with alcohol. It looked like he was laughing, or maybe he was choking.

One active seemed to be doing all the dunking—the fraternity's president, no less—so Nick pushed him away to get a better look at what was going on. Then he glanced across the room and he saw the most amazing pair of caramel eyes staring back. The girl seemed vaguely familiar—she had black hair to her shoulders, smooth skin, and suntanned cheeks—but that couldn't be right, because he sure as hell would have remembered her. She was the prettiest thing he had ever seen outside of a porn magazine. Her dark hair was smooth as glass, and she wore a cropped t-shirt that hugged her chest. He felt like he knew her already, like he knew everything about her, but that was crazy, wasn't it?

She looked worried, though. She was frowning, like maybe she wasn't having any fun with this. Her brown eyes slanted at him, as if she thought no one else should be having any fun with it, either. He knew it was up to him to get the pledge brother out of there, and just to make sure the pretty girl noticed him, he would smile at her afterward.

He didn't get his chance. The fraternity's president came back at him from the wall, both fists flying, and knocked him into the bathtub, into the muck. Tepid, grainy, thick as paste, it filled his ears, his cheeks, his nose. He panicked for a second. He couldn't swim, he couldn't even float, and liquid was everywhere.

Just when he realized he couldn't possibly breathe down there, he reared his head back and sprayed the crowd with purple punch, which sent one of the sorority girls shrieking into the hall. The pretty girl looked all wavery behind the curtain of punch in front of his eyes, so he wiped his face with the back of his hand. She was staring at the floor, at the other pledge, who had curled up like a dying dog right there on the bathroom tile. Like a shivering, sick mutt.

It was now or never. He had to do something. So he hollered for an ambulance as loud as he could. He also moved closer to where the girl stood. Maybe she'd want to talk to him after everything was over.

More than anything, he felt bad for the pledge brother rolled onto his side, because that could have been *him* lying there half-dead on the dirty bathroom tile, spitting up purple and no one thinking twice about it. No one caring if he lived or died.

But Nick did; he cared. Later, much later, when he was finally back in his dorm room, dry again, he wondered if he would have helped that guy if he hadn't spied the pretty girl in the cropped t-shirt first. But he already knew the answer. Of course he would have. It was the least he could have done. He flicked clumps of dried punch from his hair, and gazed at his reflection. No matter what, he would never tell the girl with the caramel eyes that he did it for her sake, too. He would let her think he was a hero through and through. And that was the beginning of his love affair with Rhetta Day.

The pain in his abdomen began to subside now, there in the hospital bed, and a smile weakly flittered across his face.

★ ★ ★ ★ ★

"Hello again."

The sound of the stranger's voice was so unexpected, so smooth compared to the clatter in the cafeteria, that Rhetta nearly dropped her lunch tray. She whirled around to see the doctor from the day before. Same time, same place, same brilliant smile.

Instead of hurrying away this time, Dr. Eamon McAllister grinned even more, his tanned face broadening. "Come here often?"

It was such a corny line she couldn't help but laugh. "At least once a day. You?"

He picked up his lunch tray, which held a thin sandwich cut crosswise. "Never more. C'mon." With that, he turned and took a few steps through the jumble of tables and chairs, never once glancing over his shoulder.

There was no denying the cafeteria was packed. Plus, the doctor was already a quarter of the way through the lunchroom. It was either follow him, or face the prospect of eating lunch alone again, so she decided to follow.

Awkwardly, she balanced her tray in one hand and a diet cola in the other. She could barely make out the sound of a piano medley playing over the loudspeaker as she walked along. It sounded like jazz, but who could tell with canned music?

She followed his footsteps until they both stood in front of a door marked "no entrance." Gallantly, he pushed the door open and she followed again, her eyes narrowing as they entered a cool, dark void. They were in some kind of a storage room. Not exactly the most conventional place to eat lunch, but then again, help *was* close by if the doctor turned out to be a homicidal maniac, as long as the nurses watching television in the lunchroom didn't mind abandoning their soap opera to help her.

She walked farther into the half-light. They stood in a cavernous holding area that was filled with cardboard boxes, some wooden pallets, and mismatched crates stamped "fragile." Once her eyes had adjusted, she noticed a chain-link fence segregated a small area from the rest of the room. With its soaring roof and concrete floor, the space looked exactly like a loading dock.

"How did you ever find this place?" She surveyed the piles of medical supplies and plastic-wrapped equipment, all of it slumbering under a web of dust.

"Lucky, I guess. It's a good place for a nap." He grinned at her sheepishly. "Handy when you work twenty-four hours a day."

Such a friendly face, her grandmother would say. He jabbed his finger toward a row of squat boxes clustered by the chain-link holding area. As they settled onto the tops of two of the heartiest boxes, she became conscious of the lunch tray in her hands and immediately regretted her choice. There was nothing like trying to make small talk with a good-looking man and chew lettuce at the same time. The trick was to take small bites and ask lots of questions. "You know Nick Tahari, right?" She balanced the wobbly tray on her knees as she sat down.

"Yep." Pale lines appeared at the corners of his eyes as he bit into his sandwich.

"His wife told me you went to high school together."

"Long Beach Jefferson. Go Jackrabbits." He pumped his arm in the air, half-heartedly. "Me and high school didn't always get along. Too many cliques. So, what's your name?"

"Rhetta Day." She laid her fork down and offered him her right hand. "PR flak."

"That sounds like a dangerous job."

His hand felt warm, and a few wheat kernels rubbed from his palm onto hers. "Actually, I've only been here six months. My friend called yesterday when they admitted Nick. How's he doing?"

"You know I'm not his doctor. I'm a first-year resident, or what we call a slave."

She smiled. "In a few years you'll be freed. Then you can go out and make the big bucks." The lettuce on her tray looked every bit as wilted as the day before, so she gave up and snatched a packet of crackers half-hidden by the plate.

"I don't know. I'd probably do this job even if it didn't pay so well."

"Uh-huh."

"Really. I like it." Now it was his turn to shift the tray of food on his lap, and he looked straight into her eyes. "Most patients are scared to death by the time they get to the OR. My job is to help them relax. I love anesthesia."

"Well I'll be, a conscientious doc." She dusted some crumbs from her palms. "I was beginning to feel like Dionysus, searching for a doctor who cares."

"Some of us do," he said forcefully, as if to convince both of them, "but it's hard not to burn out. You've got your rotations, your malpractice insurance, your student loans." He ticked off the items with his free hand. "Plus, every mother west of the Mississippi River trying to fix you up with her daughter."

"I wouldn't know about that." A trickle of crumbs escaped from the second packet of crackers, dirtying her cotton shirt, and she wiped them off distractedly. "My parents died when I was young."

"Oh . . . I'm sorry." He looked sorry; his eyebrows had drawn so closely together they nearly touched.

"Don't be. It happened a long time ago. My grandmother raised me." She shifted on the carton. She always felt uncomfortable discussing her family with outsiders, even good-looking ones, because people invariably said the same things and looked at her the same way. First, she'd get a sentence about the mysteries of life, then she'd be thrown a maudlin look, and—this was the worst part—the speaker usually touched her shoulder. She hated that most of all. As if she were a child again and hearing the news for the first time, instead of a grown-up woman trying to make her way in the world. "So, you knew Nick in high school?" It was best to change the subject as quickly as possible.

"Yeah, we met our junior year. What about you?"

"College. We were in a couple of classes together. I don't know. We just got to be friends." Come to think of it, most of their time together was spent at a bar on campus called The Shack, not in any classroom. That's where most friendships started or ended at Cal West. "We used to drink at this little place all the time. He could drink anyone under the table."

"And then he goes and becomes a cop. Weren't you surprised? I was."

"A little." But that was such a long time ago and so many things had happened since then.

The doctor was about to speak again when his pager shrieked, once more shattering the calm. He grimaced, and then stiffly rose. "I'm sorry, but duty calls. Can we continue this later? How 'bout lunch tomorrow?" He offered her his hand, and this time his palm felt smooth. "I may have another hiding place up my sleeve."

"Sure. Can you let me know how Nick's tests come out?"

"We'll see. By the way—" He pointed at his chin.

Quickly she wiped her jaw, which sent a telltale sprinkle of cracker crumbs floating to the ground. *So much for first impressions.* "Thanks for sharing your lunch spot, Doctor."

"Any time."

They left the cafeteria side by side, the doctor's relaxed, easygoing swagger next to her own businesslike stride. Once they got to the busy corridor, a parade of candy-colored uniforms whisked by: lime green, sky blue, sunflower yellow, even bismuth pink. When they reached the lobby, too soon, he turned and flashed that brilliant smile. She realized she had been holding her breath for the last minute or so, and finally exhaled.

Mr. Tennet's office lay at the very end of the executive corridor. Halfway back to her own office, Rhetta decided to continue on. Maybe the chief executive could help her figure out why someone would place Nick's information off-limits when there didn't seem to be a good reason to do so.

Unlike the hospital's lobby, which was raucous and bright, with a ceiling that soared two stories and windows that drank in the afternoon sun, a cloud seemed to hover over the executive's hall. Rhetta felt it the minute she stepped from the speckled linoleum of the lobby onto the Berber carpet. Rumor had it the medical director's wife had hired a famous decorator from Los Angeles to paint the walls taupe and hang expensive oil paintings there. Which didn't sit too well with the hospital's donors, who thought their money should be spent on respirators for sick babies, and not on lush oil paintings. But what could they do? So, the paintings, the polished brass fixtures, the mahogany furniture, the surround-sound stereo system fixed on a smooth jazz station; it all remained.

The seascapes blurred in her periphery as she walked. The hall even had its own elevator, for heaven's sake, designed to segregate the executives from the unwashed masses in the lobby. She never rode in it unless she had to, and even then she made faces at a video camera in the corner to give the security guard something to laugh about.

Now, she silently prayed Mr. Tennet would be in his office, and alone. While the hospital's chief executive always welcomed her warmly, with a fatherly gaze and a gentle handshake, his administrative assistant did not. For some reason, the assistant disliked Rhetta, and had from the very start. Maybe he was jealous of Rhetta's daughterly relationship with the CEO. The guy looked to be about her age—twenty-nine—and maybe he envied her. Who knew? The few times she'd asked him for an appointment, he had said the chief executive was much too busy for that. Could she maybe come back tomorrow? It went on like that for days, until finally, Rhetta gave up and typed out an email instead. But this wasn't the kind of thing she could trust to a computer. No, for this she needed to see the CEO in person.

Thankfully, the assistant's chair was empty. She peeked through the door of Mr. Tennet's office, and there he sat, on the phone, behind a battered partner's desk made of wide oak planks and brass studs, as if it belonged in Jackson Hole, Wyoming, and not in Southern California. Not for him the fancy antiques carved from gleaming mahogany. She smiled at the thought of the famous Los Angeles decorator fuming about the unusual decor.

The CEO glanced up when she entered, and then cupped his hand around the receiver. "Might be a spell," he told her in a stage whisper. "Get comfortable."

He waved the phone at a stuffed leather armchair placed cater-corner to the desk. She gratefully accepted the invitation and slid onto cool leather. Mr. Tennet was almost seventy years old now, and white hair fluttered around his face like tufts of ripe cotton. Her first day on the job, a human resources rep had called him St. Tennet, and it was only half in jest. But Mr. Tennet wasn't like any of the saints she knew. Not in his bolo tie, perpetually skewed, or in those scuffed cowboy boots, which added another inch to his already large frame.

No, saints were towering figures in stained-glass windows who watched her during Mass. She hadn't been to church in years, but she remembered how small she felt under the ominous figures in their flowing robes. Mr. Tennet seemed more sinner than saint to her, like Peter in the Garden of Gethsemane, captured in a window in the vestibule, or Samson letting Delilah cut off his hair in a picture from the Old Testament.

Maybe that's why she liked him so much. With him, she didn't have to pretend to be anything she wasn't. He accepted her wholly and had from the start.

Finally, he swung his boot off the desk and hung up the telephone. "Good to see you, Rhetta. What brings you here?"

Where to begin? Ever since Nick had been admitted, something had felt wrong. A gunshot wound, a punctured lung, a fractured collarbone, all of those things she could wrap her mind around, no questions asked. But an accidental poisoning? That was too nebulous. The words held no weight. "A friend of mine was admitted Monday. It's been horrible. I keep thinking that maybe if I see his medical record, everything else will make sense."

Mr. Tennet didn't move. Instead, he studied the Navaho rug peeking out from under his desk, suddenly interested in its bright pattern. "I wish I could help you out," he finally answered. "But no one gets to see those records. Not even me."

Didn't he know this was different? Didn't he realize they were talking about Nick? "Please, Mr. Tennet."

"Ask me something else. How's your parking space working out? Want something closer?" His eyes implored her to change her mind.

But she didn't want a new parking space, damn it; she wanted to see Nick's electronic chart. She closed her eyes rather than look at him. "Just once. I won't ask you again. I'll look at it and close out of the program. No one has to know."

"We'll know, Rhetta. You and me. Look, why don't you take a day off and get some rest. Maybe after you've had a chance to think about it . . ."

Sullenly, she opened her eyes. "No." Twenty-four hours away from the hospital wasn't going to change a thing. She could no more drive away from Nick right now than she could have pitched a rock through one of those beautiful stained-glass windows at church. "I only thought . . . forget I asked." She rose from the seat and began to rake her fingers through her hair. There had to be a way to get her hands on Nick's record. It was only a matter of figuring out the *right* way.

CHAPTER 4

Cold. It was so cold. Nick longed to pull the wafer-thin blanket higher on his chest, but his fingers wouldn't cooperate. When he tried to clench his fist nothing happened, so he gave up, exhausted by the effort. How long had he been asleep? It seemed like forever since they had wheeled him into the hospital room and placed him smack-dab in the middle of machines that flashed and buzzed and whirred through the day and night.

This wasn't a good sign—a private room—he knew that. They didn't just hand out private rooms like candy. Something must be really wrong with him to rate so much space. And so much attention. Strangers in lab coats constantly leaned over him. They poked at his arms, his chest, even his eyes, like he was a slab of meat on a counter; like he wasn't even there.

Maybe he *wasn't* really here. Maybe this was a bad dream and any second now he'd wake up with his dog at his feet and Rhetta a phone call away. That was how it went down before he woke up in the middle of this snowstorm of white. White walls, white ceiling, white sleeves. White everywhere.

Couldn't they at least have found a color television set? The one suspended over his bed flickered gray and white all day long, like another heart monitor. Someone had turned the sound off, which was just as well.

His head lolled against the pillow. Even the smells were different here. Sharp disinfectant and overcooked vegetables, rubbing alcohol and urine samples trapped in plastic cups. Sweat, sometimes, from a body leaning over his bed. They could wipe away the color from his room easily enough, but they couldn't get rid of the smells.

He wanted to go home. Maybe if he could push the call button next to his bed, he'd explain to a nurse that he didn't belong there. He would rest just as well in his recliner at home. He didn't know what kind of bug had worked its slimy way into his system, but he'd lick this.

He rolled onto his side and something sharp pulled at his wrist. If he could reach the amber light next to his bed he could make them understand. He didn't have time to be lying around like this. He knew it was midafternoon from the angle of the shadows; approximately three o'clock. Estimation was his favorite section on the police academy exam, and he was good at it. He could guess the number of people in a room at a glance, give or take a few. Now, hard shadows on the floor told him it was halfway to nightfall. He should buckle on his holster and get his head straight for another night on the streets.

He and his partner, Larry, would cruise all over the Valley in their panda. Early on, in the quiet hours, they would trade stories that rambled like the narrow side streets. As night fell, though, they both knew the police scanner could break in at any second, so the jokes got shorter and shorter. They'd sprint to a punch line, then swap a sweating soft drink like runners in a relay passing a baton back and forth.

Sometimes Larry would splash soda on the steering wheel, which used to make their captain crazy when he saw the inside of their unit all messed up. That's what the crimson call button next to his bed reminded him of now. The squad car. The glowing light on the radio. It was their lifeline back to the police station and someone who actually cared about whether they came back from patrol in one piece. Hell, the locals didn't care. They'd just as soon have him and Larry disappear into a manhole. Leave them alone to fight over their drugs like a pack of wild dogs.

One push and dispatch would answer him. Would guide him home again. Maybe if he could reach the crimson light next to his bed, he'd hear the sweet, sweet voice of dispatch.

He tried to roll further. The needle pinched his arm, but he didn't cry out. It was so close, he could feel the pull of it. This is what it felt like inside the squad car when the seatbelt held him back, kept him from reaching the glowing red light on the ceiling.

Only a little bit more and he would be home free. He strained with everything he had, sweat streaming down his face, but the metal side rail held him back; it wouldn't let him through, no matter how hard he leaned. Tears of frustration sprang to his eyes. Why wouldn't they let him call dispatch? Dispatch would know how to bring him home again.

He fell back to the bed, back to the cold sterile sheet that chafed like sandpaper. He wanted to go home. He didn't belong here. He belonged back in his family room with Jet's muzzle under his fingers and Rhetta's sweet, sweet voice on the other end of the telephone.

He clenched his fist, and this time his fingers worked. He swiped at the needle in his arm and yanked it out with everything he had. With a pop, the needle pulled free, trailing blood as it dangled from his hand. He wanted to go home. If they wouldn't let him call dispatch he'd have to do it himself. He willed his legs to rise, willed them to swing up and over the metal bar, but that was too much. They wouldn't budge. He would work on that tomorrow. *That was it.* He'd work on getting his legs up and over the bed. From there, it would be ten-and-a-half feet to the door and another twenty-four feet—twenty-four-point-five, tops—to the elevator. To the beautiful, glowing buttons of the elevator.

Maybe if he closed his eyes, he'd be strong enough to try again. Dispatch would still be there when he woke up. Dispatch would know how to bring him home again.

"You've got a bunch of messages." Wanda looked up from the compact mirror lying open on her desk and waved a hot pink mascara tube toward a plastic holder. The slots were labeled with names, most of them empty, except for Rhetta's, which bulged with slips of pale blue paper. Her meeting with Mr. Tennet couldn't have lasted more than ten minutes; lunch with the doctor, another twenty.

"Nice to see you, too." She reached over to pluck the messages from the box and inhaled a nose-full of stale cigarette smoke mixed with drugstore perfume. Wanda must have spent her lunch break with the operating room nurses again, smoking outside the surgery wing. The hiding spot was on the ground level, no less, where patients and families could walk right by as the staff puffed away. That was Wanda—hard and soft—unfiltered cigarettes and flowery perfume.

"Most of them are from the same guy. He sounded kinda desperate."

"Really?" Rhetta riffled through the stack, where page after page listed the same name on the first line: Officer Larry Belknap. By the fourth message, the name had been shortened to Larry B., and a few pages later, to Larry. Wanda's handwriting grew more lax with each message, and by the final note the ink slipped sideways as if it were falling off the page.

"Why would he call me here?"

Wanda had resumed her work with the mascara tube, her mouth agape, and was too engrossed to respond.

The last time she'd spoken with Officer Belknap had been years earlier, when she had returned to her apartment after meeting up with friends at The Corner Pocket. Nick had joined them later that night, his left eye bandaged tight, all bluster and swagger about how he and Larry had been ambushed by a street gang while on patrol.

She remembered the way her chest gradually tightened as Nick told her about that night. She had perched on a barstool, air eking from her lungs, and had promised herself that she would call his police partner as soon as she got home, to find out what had really happened that night in South Central.

She remembered Larry's voice: a sonorous baritone that instantly quelled her fears. Nick had once described him as a large African-American, bald, with an addiction to diet cola and corn chips. When she finally reached him at the station, he told her that Nick was a hero that night, and she didn't doubt it. Since that time, nothing had changed with Larry, as far as she knew. He was still on the force, still working with Nick, at least before the accident, and still as hefty as ever.

She turned away from Wanda and stepped into her office, flicking on the overheads as she went. The office was as spartan as some of the hospital units: a laminate-topped desk, metal file cabinet under a picture window, two side chairs with silver arms. But she had dressed up the place with a seascape that hung over her desk, and if she tilted her head just right, she could imagine what it felt like to stroll along the roiling surf. She often sought refuge in the watercolor when she had fistfuls of messages from anxious callers and nothing much to tell them.

Now, she tossed the telephone messages on the desk and plopped into an armchair tucked into the kneehole. She reached for the telephone, and dialed the number for the police department, her foot tapping the floor as she waited through two rings before the familiar, sonorous voice answered. "Officer Belknap? It's Rhetta Day. You called?" The line fell silent for a minute, and Rhetta wondered whether they accidentally had been disconnected. "Hello?"

"Yes. I'm here." A tight laugh sounded through the receiver. "This is something, isn't it? My partner's in the hospital and I haven't had a chance to see him. How's he doin'?"

Rhetta leaned back, relieved to be talking to someone who didn't want a technical diagnosis, who didn't care about mitochondrial potential or respiratory distress, who only wanted to be able to understand in the simplest terms possible what was wrong with his friend. "They've got him in ICU. He's on full oxygen right now so he can't speak."

"Really?" A long, low whistle floated over the telephone line. "Nothin' at all?"

"Nope. He's using notes, though." It was terribly ironic that Nick, who told stories better than anyone else she knew, wasn't able to speak now. It was ironic, and it broke her heart.

"So you haven't talked to him at all?"

"I went up yesterday and he was awake. Groggy, but awake."

"Hmmm. Say, by any chance did he ever mention me? You know, tell you anything about him and me last weekend?"

Rhetta stared at the telephone. Before Nick was admitted to the hospital, they hadn't talked about anything more serious than his rec league basketball game. The only time he had ever talked to her about Larry was in the middle of some long-winded story, and Larry always played sidekick to Nick's comedian. He did mention once that Larry didn't like to play by the rules, or something like that, and that he would rather act first and ask permission later. But that was weeks ago, long before Nick was admitted.

"No, nothing at all. By the way, how'd you get my number?"

Larry chuckled. "You were no secret. Nick talked about you all the time. Said you worked in public relations at the hospital. I just thought you might know something . . . you might have heard something." His voice sounded breezy now, as if a big weight had been lifted from his shoulders. Very different from the start of their call.

"Well, I wish I could tell you more. You should come up to see him. I'm sure he'd love it."

"Oh yeah, that. Well, me and hospitals don't get along. Let me know if anything changes, will you? Let me know if they take out that oxygen thingamajig."

"Of course. Well, good-bye." She hung up the telephone slowly, pondering the change in Larry's tone. He had started off so tentative, but by the time they were through speaking, he sounded positively upbeat. She considered the pile of messages, lost in thought. There were thirteen ice-blue notes, ten of them from Larry. For someone who only wanted to touch base on his partner, who wanted a brief update with not much more than the sketchiest of details, that seemed rather excessive.

Wanda peeked around the doorjamb, looking like a startled doe with her eyes ringed in black. "I forgot to tell you something. Arianna wants to see you. Stat."

Rhetta groaned and pushed aside the messages. If Wanda was a little bit tacky, and she was, her boss was the opposite. Smooth as plastic, Arianna Brouchard lived in expensive designer suits that would have cost Wanda a whole paycheck. Something tweed for Monday morning meetings, an Italian designer by midweek, and then a daring deconstructed pantsuit by Friday. Early on, Rhetta decided that Arianna must have been raised on the wrong side of town, so she tried to make up for it with fancy clothes. Like the way she wore four-inch heels, when she couldn't have been more than five feet tall. Or, the way she sprayed her hair into submission—made it so brittle it would crack with one poke—confirmed for Rhetta that she was overcompensating for something.

She also knew that as far as Arianna Brouchard was concerned, no news was the best news. Better to stay out of the woman's way altogether than risk being asked to do another project Arianna thought was beneath her. For some reason, Arianna acted like the hospital's patients were an inconvenience. She talked about the building's "census," as if the beds were filled with widgets, and not flesh and blood. Quotas, revenue projections, return on investment, that was Arianna. She was so much better suited for a job with a consumer products company, high-tech or maybe aerospace, but Arianna would never admit that.

"Thanks, Wanda." She rose from the desk and walked toward her boss's door. Arianna sat behind an imposing desk, with windows on all sides. It was a plum corner office reserved for the vice president of marketing She wore a conservative tweed suit today, with a strand of oversized pearls big as abacus beads, only white, and cinched with a gossamer bow.

"Come in, Rhetta," she said without rising. "Sit down." She pointed to a chair placed in front of the desk, which had chrome handles and expensive lavender fabric. *Here we go again.*

"Something's happened. We might have a little, uh, indiscretion on our hands."

Rhetta winced. "Tell me it's not our favorite neonatologist." One of the hospital's doctors had somehow gotten hold of the intercom the month before, and had warbled "My Funny Valentine" to a special pediatric nurse. Dead drunk. A respiratory tech finally wrested the microphone away from him by the end of the first stanza. Why the doctor felt the need to broadcast his affection for his coworker to the entire hospital was beyond her. More troubling, how could they explain a doctor who was drunk at two o'clock in the afternoon? Turned out, the man was exhausted from his caseload—that was the official reason anyway—and the hospital bigwigs sent him home for a week of bed rest.

"No, it's not him. Though I still don't think that man is in treatment." Arianna stroked the oversized beads languidly. "It's something even more dangerous. If it gets out, we could all look *vary, vary* bad."

On top of everything else, Arianna spoke in an exaggerated Southern drawl, which seemed to come and go depending on whether she was angry or not. The more agitated she became, and that was happening a lot lately, the heavier the accent. Wanda swore the vice president was faking it.

"She says she's from 'New Or-le-ans,' plain as day," Wanda would huff after hearing Arianna introduce herself to someone new. Wanda sometimes vacationed in southern Louisiana, near the Texas border, and she would bring in plastic dishes filled with crawfish etouffee and real Cajun gumbo that smelled so good wafting out of the break room. "Why, everybody who's anybody knows it's 'N'awlins.' " Wanda had even invited Arianna to a crawfish boil once, just to be neighborly, which, of course, Arianna had declined.

Now Arianna leaned forward and drummed her fingers on her mahogany desk. "You know Dr. Visser? Dr. Jeremy Visser?" Her eyes widened when she pronounced the last name.

"Of course. What did he do?" Dr. Visser was a surgeon, mid-forties, distinguished-looking though completely bald, which somehow looked right on him. He was good at translating complicated medical terms for the media. No, he was *great* at it. Didn't matter whether he was discussing a new transplant procedure, the latest endoscope, the new surgery suites—which were named after him, of course—he was at the front of every reporter's Rolodex, the V in his last name notwithstanding. After a while, the nurses started calling him "Doc Hollywood" to his face, and it was a compliment.

"He operated on a city councilman four days ago. Very simple. Nuthin' to it." Arianna leaned back and casually waved her hand. She should have been an actress, really. She would have given any movie star a run for her money. " 'Cept he took out the wrong kidney."

"That's horrible." Rhetta leaned back, too. "How can that be?"

"Turns out we have a nurse who swears the doctor was doing drugs. Cocaine, she thinks. High as a kite." Arianna swiveled her chair around to look out the oversized window, which framed a line of cars that came and left through the hospital's security gate. "Not the first time, either."

"You've got to be kidding." St. James was so big, anybody could say anything about a person and it was scout's honor, most times. But, still, there had to have been other people in the operating room. A surgeon would be surrounded by two or three more nurses, plus technicians, and always the anesthesiologist. It was a regular party in the OR most times. "Who else knows about this?"

"No one, yet. 'Cept I don't see how we can keep it a secret." Arianna stared at her, whatever mock sweetness she had feigned at the beginning quickly dissolving. It was clear now that Arianna didn't want her to find a witness at all. That was *not* why she had summoned Rhetta to her office. "I expect you to put a lid on this." Sure enough, out came the shades of melodrama.

"Don't worry. I'll see what I can do." First up would be to call the hospital's legal department. She'd see if the councilman's family already had hired an attorney. Maybe she'd make a visit to the OR and speak with the nurses. Explore every angle, even twice. She couldn't wait to leave Arianna's office and get on with it, so she ducked through the doorway and crossed over to where Wanda sat typing with a fluffy headed troll doll that perched on her computer monitor.

"What's up?" Wanda tried her best to look nonchalant as she typed.

"Can't say."

The assistant frowned. "What about a hint?"

"Look, this is important. If any reporters call today, put them right through to me. As far as you know, nothing's going on."

"Yeah, right," she said. "Don't worry, I won't say anything."

Now that would be a miracle. Rhetta continued to walk to her own office, which was only half as big as Arianna's, but it, too, had a window. Her view, unlike Arianna's vista, was dominated by the patient care tower, all stucco and reflected glass.

She opened her desk drawer and rummaged around for a rail-thin telephone directory with curled edges. After finding it, she flipped open the front cover. Quickly, her finger trailed down a list of telephone extensions and halfway down the page she found what she was looking for: the operating room . . . extension two-one. She dialed two-one, and then waited through a few rings.

"Nurses' station," a voice finally answered.

"Hi, this is Rhetta Day, up in PR. I need something off the surgery log."

"Just a sec. Gotta get my supervisor."

Static from a paging system sounded in the background and, after a minute, a new voice spoke into the telephone. "This is Dorothy. Can I help you?"

"Yes, I hope so. I need to check something on the surgery log."

"Hold on—who is this?"

"Sorry. I'm Rhetta Day, from the PR department. Can you check the schedule for me?"

"I guess." The woman sounded unsure.

"It was a kidney removal, a few days ago. The surgeon was Visser."

Fingernails clicked against a keyboard. "Here it is. Looks like it was Thursday." Rhetta heard more clicks in the background. "Dr. Visser operated in suite five. Is that all you need?"

"Not quite." Rhetta picked up a ballpoint pen. She scribbled "Thursday, suite five" across a block on her desktop calendar. "I need to know the names of the OR nurses."

"Lucky for you we log everyone in." She heard more taps in the background. "We had three nurses there. Are you ready? Vandermeer, Ray, and Copley."

"Great." Rhetta scrawled the names of the nurses across the very bottom of the calendar. "If you had to pick, who works with Visser the most?"

The woman sighed. "Can you tell me what this is about? The unit's a zoo right now."

"Sure. We got a patient complaint." Which was a lie, but it was close enough.

"Well, Copley's been here the longest. She probably knows the docs better than anyone." The supervisor paused. "Course, Vandermeer's been here a long time, too. But if it's public relations, she's probably not your best choice. No, I'd go with Copley."

How odd. Most nursing supervisors completely supported their staffs, every last one of them, no doubt because of the twelve-hour workdays and the amount of grief they got from the doctors. "What's wrong with Vandermeer?"

"Let's say she's not the happiest person in the world. Frankly, I think Susannah's a little burnt out."

Rhetta wrote a name onto the pad, and then absentmindedly tapped the bottom of the ballpoint against the desk. "Is Vandermeer working today?"

"I told you, she's probably not your best choice." The woman sounded put-off now. "But I suppose she's around here somewhere."

"Thanks. By the way, a friend of mine was admitted yesterday. I'd like to find out how he's doing. How can I do that?"

The supervisor chortled. "Your best bet is to ask someone

from pharmacy. They hold all the power here. Didn't anyone ever tell you that?"

"Really? No kidding. Well, thanks for your trouble." Rhetta twisted her wrist as she hung up the receiver and brought her watch's face into view. The small hand was fast approaching three o'clock. She'd have to hurry if she wanted to catch the OR nurse, and then hunt down someone from the pharmacy department.

CHAPTER 5

As Nick slept in his room, moments of clarity flashed through the fog. He lay on a hard bed now. He wasn't in the fraternity house anymore, toweling dry his hair, thinking about a pretty girl named Rhetta Day, or hoping to hear the sweet, sweet voice of dispatch over the radio scanner. Now, strange voices swirled, sometimes loud, sometimes not, and one time a burst of light popped when someone pried open his left eyelid. Still, on the whole, he had never slept so soundly in his life. Even when he awoke, however briefly, he turned his head and drifted off again. Whatever they were feeding him through the tube they had reinserted in his arm—of that much he was aware—he wanted more of it.

Memories pinballed around in his skull as he fell fast asleep. He was back in his senior year of college now, and graduation was still a few weeks away. He had long ago figured out that frat pledges took the best notes. So, one day, when the noon sun sat smack overhead, he decided to lure Rhetta to The Shack for a cold one with the promise of free tacos for lunch . . . knowing that his fraternity buddies would cover for him in econ class.

They all ended up at The Shack anyway; he was just cutting to the chase. Sitting there in the semi-dark, with Rhetta across the table, there was nowhere else he'd rather be. And her wearing a low-cut white tank top with frayed blue jean shorts. He remembered the smell of coconut suntan lotion, and the way the ends of her black hair glistened. If he thought about her taking a shower, back in her dorm room, rubbing shampoo into her hair and smoothing body wash over her shoulders, he would lose it. So he gripped his beer bottle harder. Today was the day he would say something. Today was the day he would make his move.

The sight of some new freckles on the bridge of her nose distracted him, though. She must have gone to the beach again over the weekend, to the sliver of sand between lifeguard towers four and five. They knew each other well enough to know their schedules.

Every once in a while, as he studied her pretty face, some joker would swing open The Shack's front door and he had to look away, like a mole exposed to daylight at the edge of its burrow. The door was only plywood, splintered from staples of motocross posters and roommate-wanted flyers, and the yellow ferns between the booths were fake, but that only made it better. There was nothing to break, nothing to steal, nothing to worry about. There was nothing to do but sit there all afternoon and tell stories and listen to Rhetta laugh.

So he decided to tell her a funny story; the serious stuff could wait until the next beer. Every once in a while, he paused and checked out a row of black and white pictures that hung on the bar's wall, he remembered. The photos were of people doing exactly the same thing—drinking beer with lazy smiles, whiling away a spring afternoon—only the people flash-frozen wore buzzed flattops, furry sideburns, or punky spikes, depending on which decade they came from.

He twirled a plastic ashtray around once or twice with his finger while he spoke to her. The leprechaun green lettering, fancy lettering, like on a diploma, blurred as he thought about what he would say next. She was so easy to talk to, he didn't think much about it. He didn't have to do anything but be himself. Didn't matter that he'd barely graduate. Didn't matter no one thought he'd make it through the police academy. Didn't matter he couldn't slam dunk anymore. Rhetta didn't care.

So, he began to ramble about the academy, about his mom— anything to loosen her up before he got to the tough stuff— when she leaned across the table and picked up a bottle cap. Just breathing in her suntan lotion shut him up good. She took the shiny cap and started to scratch something into the table, but she had to work at it, and her shoulders hunched forward and there was her cleavage. It was all he could do to keep his hands around the beer bottle's neck and watch her shove the cap into water-stained wood.

A rough R appeared, upside down, only she couldn't quite get it to go around in the varnish, so it looked more like a K. Even before she started in on the D, he knew she was carving her initials into the table. As she worked, the tip of her tongue appeared between her front teeth, all pink and wet, until he thought he'd pop the neck right off that beer bottle.

When she was finally through carving her initials, she lowered her hand about an inch and scratched out a small plus sign, then a big N.

She was carving his initials into the table, too. *Their* initials into the table. Just like that, outta the blue, what he had been waiting for.

He couldn't stop grinning, he remembered that much. He had waited so long. All those times he had buddied up to her at the campus bookstore, at frat house parties, at Java Junction, checking out at the grocery store, when he wanted to wrap his arm around her and claim her for himself.

His waiting finally was paying off. Here, in The Shack, with one beer down and a few more to go. When she finished carving the N, she lowered the bottle cap and deliberately traced out a lopsided O.

Only, she wasn't supposed to do that. She was supposed to

scratch his initials, right there, right under her name. It was supposed to be a T, not an O. How could she make that mistake?

She might as well have kicked him in the stomach. The beer bottle slipped from his hand, and before he could move, it crashed to the ground; shards, splinters everywhere. Yellow suds foamed on the tabletop and covered up the letters. She stared at him, her moist lips pursed, and he knew that she understood. She understood what had happened.

"I was gonna write no one," she whispered. He remembered he tried to hand her a wad of cocktail napkins, but she ignored them. "C'mon Nick—the police academy? You're gonna get yourself killed!" Finally, she had taken the napkins from him, but she was angry, and she had slapped them hard onto the table.

She'd already knocked the wind out of him and he couldn't speak. Couldn't do anything but watch sudsy rivulets of beer tumble over the side, drip onto his jeans, and then splatter his flip-flops. He had no idea she wanted him to choose between being a cop and being with her. It wouldn't have been a tough choice. Not really. Not if she had given him time to think about it.

He would have chosen her in a heartbeat. But he'd already committed to the academy and the police sergeant expected him there the next month. The brass had even sent a fancy letter to his house, which his mom immediately framed and hung by the front door. He couldn't tell her that he'd changed his mind; that it was all a big mistake. He couldn't do that to his mom. Besides, he had everything worked out. He was going to be a cop—a great one, too—and Rhetta would be a public relations whiz. Just like she'd planned, just like he'd hoped. He'd come home at night to her and her big, beautiful smile, and if she was too tired to cook for him, they'd go out for pizza, or Chinese, or whatever the hell she wanted. He'd sit across from her in a vinyl booth at the Red Dragon and thank his lucky stars that she was all his. He had it all worked out. They made a great team; a perfect pair. It was all part of his plan. Didn't she know that?

His stomach ached. Worse than that, he wanted to cry. As the memory faded, as the door to The Shack opened and closed for a final time, as the smell of coconut suntan lotion and spilled beer and cracked peanut shells disappeared, he found himself back in a sterile hospital room. Back to the smells of overcooked vegetables and disinfectant. His body jerked, just once, on the intractable hospital bed, and pain rippled through him.

CHAPTER 6

A little before three o'clock, Rhetta walked to the hospital's stairwell and took the steps two at a time, until she reached the ground floor. She exited the building and stood in the doctors' parking lot . . . a blacktopped square that chomped into the southeast corner of the patient care tower. Heat radiated off the pavement like silver steam that undulated across the parking spaces and was pushed along by the tail end of an ocean breeze that had to have originated a good five miles away.

The parking lot abutted the surgery suites. It was meant for the doctors who arrived at five o'clock most mornings and were always running late. It had become, much to the hospital administrator's chagrin, the unofficial "social club," the only place where chain smokers could commiserate and puff away.

It was an odd sight. A group of mostly women clustered just outside a heavy, rivet-studded door, at all hours of the day, still wearing paper shower caps and elasticized booties from surgery. They were nearly indistinguishable from each other in their baggy, army-green scrubs and tennis shoes, and they gestured sporadically with glowing nubs when they weren't crossing their arms and looking at each other sideways. She felt sorry for them on winter days, when they desperately cupped their lighters and nursed tiny fires, and then stomped their tennis shoes to stay warm. No chance of that today.

A humid breeze ruffled her skirt and tickled her knees. There weren't many cars on the lot this late in the afternoon; just a luxury SUV over there next to a shiny gray sports car. A squatty, lime green electric car, which had to belong to a first-year resident—they were so idealistic that way—was parked in the very far corner. One time, a doctor drove a ninety-thousand-dollar convertible onto the lot, but he paid an X-ray tech to move it before the sun could damage its sparkling paint job.

A handful of nurses, no more than six, tops, were out today, huddled together in a triangle of shade provided by the patient care tower. They reminded Rhetta of the stoners who used to sneak out behind her high-school gym on Friday nights, usually after halftime, when the crowd had gone back to their seats. The kids had probably prayed for overtime, which would give them ten more minutes for the sweet smell of pot to dissipate. Maybe they thought their parents wouldn't notice. Just like the nurses thought patients couldn't smell cigarette smoke imbedded in their scrubs and hair, but they were both wrong.

She walked across the blacktop toward a middle-aged nurse who squatted on a concrete block. A rumpled soda can rolled drunkenly in front of her in a wavering line of red that bobbed up and down. It plinked against the pavement once, twice, three times. "Hey." That should have done it, but the woman didn't answer her. "Sure is hot."

Finally, the nurse looked up at her and squinted. "Yeah, guess so." She inhaled deeply from the glowing nub in her fingers, the skin around her mouth puckering like crinkled rice paper.

"I'm looking for someone." The chatter behind Rhetta died away as, one by one, the women fell silent. She could hear engines shifting gear on the boulevard beyond them, grinding away in a low moan. Before she could speak again, though, the door to the surgery suite swung open and a man ambled out. He was pulling a pack of cigarettes from his back pocket as he walked. The guy's face looked familiar. Familiar, but unexpected.

She hadn't seen Carlos Cervantes, Nick's old fraternity president, in ages. She couldn't help but stare, there in the hot parking lot, surrounded by cigarette smoke.

The last time she saw Carlos, they stood in a fraternity house at the start of freshman year. The place wasn't really a fraternity house, she remembered. Not like the tumbledown mansions you see in movies, with Roman columns and a pitched roof. This was a seventies duplex, old-fashioned, with brown stucco walls and an even-browner trim. They had only called it a "house" to make the fraternity sound legitimate. The duplex had a balcony out back, and she used to hold her breath whenever someone with a long-neck beer would wobble drunkenly over to that rusted-out railing.

The frat members had stapled travel posters to the wall, crooked, for a party that night. It was supposed to be a Hawaiian luau, so they had even hung a fake palm tree with drooping fronds from the dimpled ceiling. When she first arrived, a skinny kid hanging out by the fridge offered her a beer, and she accepted it. She would wait a few minutes, and then search for a friend. But a noise erupted at the back of the duplex, so she took the drink, and then wandered over to where a tight group of people had packed into the bathroom.

Someone, probably the fraternity's actives, had hijacked a claw-footed porcelain bathtub, smack in the middle of the room, and had turned it into a giant punch bowl. A film of purple punch washed with grain alcohol floated on top. It was an old trick to get girls to drink the punch before they realized there was one-hundred-ninety-proof alcohol hidden underneath it. Only, instead of slurping the mix, Carlos Cervantes had grabbed a pledge by his hair, and was shoving him, face down, into the goo. The stuff oozed into the kid's shirt, ran down his front, and puddled around his knees. He looked like a heaving purple Smurf. It was horrible. Everyone—actives and pledges alike—

had packed into the bathroom, laughing as if it was the funniest thing they had ever seen. One, two, three, dunk. The pledge started to choke on goo and his own spit, but that didn't stop Carlos from dunking him. He should have known better—he was a premed student, after all—but he didn't stop until Nick Tahari walked in, took one look, grabbed Carlos by the shoulders, and slammed him hard against the tile wall.

It grew so quiet in the room, you could hear the air flow. Come to think of it, that was the first time she realized she could easily fall for someone like Nick . . . so brave and gutsy.

Now, there was no mistaking Carlos, even in his ill-fitting lab coat. Once handsome and cocksure, president of the largest and most prestigious fraternity at Cal West, he shuffled through the door and onto the blacktop like an old man wearing bedroom slippers.

When he finally looked up, he seemed startled to see her, too. He glanced furtively from her face to the group of nurses, who were as silent as stones, as if he had been caught doing something wrong.

"Carlos?" She thought he might ignore her and keep walking, so she waved as well.

"Rhetta, right?" His smile was tight, forced. He stopped in front of her. She immediately recognized the sallow skin and hollow eyes of an alcoholic. Nothing good must have befallen him once he left college.

She'd heard about the suicide attempt. After the Pan-Hellenic Council voted to expel him for the incident with the pledge and the tubful of grain alcohol, no decent university would take him, so the story went, and he tried to end it off the beach's pier late one night. If it wasn't for a lingering surfer, he might have sunk to the ocean floor without a word. After that it was only a matter of time before he got a technician's degree online and went to work for a hospital. She didn't know which hospital, until now. "What have you been up to?" As if she hadn't heard.

"This and that. I'm in radiology." He shuffled his foot again. "It sucks. What about you?"

"PR department. I heard you worked at a hospital. Small world, right?"

"Yeah." He managed to smile this time, and the dirty whites of his eyes disappeared into a patchwork of wrinkles. For a second, the past fell away, and she glimpsed the carefree fraternity president he used to be. Cocky and proud, convinced nothing bad would ever happen, at least not to him.

"Hey, did you hear about Nick? He's here, in ICU." She couldn't imagine that Carlos wouldn't know. Word spread so quickly among the alumnae.

"Yeah. Something, isn't it? They expected me to work on him. Like that was going to happen."

She tilted her head, not quite understanding his tone, or his words. "What do you mean?"

"Funny how things turn out. Me and him again. And me just happening to work ER the night they brought him in. I mean, what were the chances? Yep, it's downright ironic, if you ask me." With that, Carlos slid the cigarettes back into his pocket, and turned to leave. "I don't need a smoke anyway. The stuff'll kill you." He grinned, a sallow, lopsided grin, and then pulled open the rivet-studded door. As quickly as he had entered her life again, with his smug smile and his puzzling words . . . he was gone.

"Don't pay any attention to him." It was the skinny nurse on the concrete block, and her words brought Rhetta back to the present. The woman must have watched the whole thing. "That guy's a little shit. What do you need?"

The speaker had a rust-colored tendril of hair plastered against her forehead. It took Rhetta a moment to find her voice.

"I'm looking for Susannah. Susannah Vandermeer."

The nurse paused and flicked a still-smoking cigarette to the ground, where it joined a dozen others, all sprinkled over the pavement like dirty confetti. She yanked the cap on her head free and layers of rusty curls fell over her shoulders, covering the one, sweat-soaked ringlet. "That's me."

"Can I talk to you?"

The nurse glanced around, and then shrugged. She rose and walked a few steps, until she was bathed in sunlight. "So talk," she said.

Rhetta crossed her arms and followed, until they stood maybe a foot apart. The woman wasn't middle-aged, after all: she could see that now. More like in her late twenties, just like her. "I talked to your supervisor."

The nurse rolled her eyes. "You poor thing." She pulled the damp ringlet on her forehead taut, then released it, and it limped back into place. "Look, I don't have much time. Do you need something?"

So much for small talk. "Yeah. I heard you assisted Dr. Visser the other day. With a kidney removal."

"You bet. First one there." She lowered her voice. "He shouldn't have been in surgery. He was climbing the walls. I could tell." Her eyes had hardened and stern lines appeared like brackets around her mouth. "But I don't need trouble."

The nurse turned to leave, and Rhetta blurted out the first thought—the only thought—that came to her. "Got a cigarette?"

"You're kidding, right?" The woman looked like she had just been asked for a million dollars. Slowly, she bent and retrieved a crushed white box from inside the paper covering her shoe. The cellophane looked shredded around the flip-top, but it was clearly a box of menthol cigarettes. Filtered, hallelujah. Susannah, still crouched, drew out a cigarette, the next-to-last one, and held it up for Rhetta. "All yours."

"Thanks." Now what? It had to be a hundred degrees and sunlight ricocheted off the sports car, the cola can, the cellophane. Echoes of Carlos's words still rang in her ears, which was distracting enough.

"No problem." The nurse shifted her weight and reached into the other paper bootie, where she withdrew a pink lighter. "Everything in there but the kitchen sink," she said.

Rhetta accepted the lighter and palmed the plastic. "What about the others? The anesthesiologist was there, right?" She flipped it open and sparked a flame. When she finally took a puff and dry smoke filled her mouth, her throat closed against the heat, so she quickly blew it out again. No one said she had to inhale.

"Yeah, I think it was an anesthesiology resident." She looked confused. "Least I'm pretty sure it was."

"Susannah!" Another nurse called to her from the triangle of shade. "We're gonna be late again."

The woman nodded, and swiped at the ringlet stalled on her forehead. "Gotta go. Wish I could be more help. And don't let that Carlos guy get to you. We all think he's mental."

A short while later, when Rhetta returned to her office, bright sun no longer streamed through the windows, which faced east. Now it was up to fluorescent tubes to take over, and they cast a green pall across the file cabinets and computer equipment, the closed office doors, the nubby walls of the newcomers' cubicles. Wanda's desk served as epicenter for the cubicles. There was definitely a hierarchy in place, and managers, like Rhetta, were given the privilege of both a door that closed and a desk that locked, while junior employees had to make do with open air and no secrets.

By this time of day, most everyone would be too burnt out to do more than return a few phone calls, maybe book an appointment, or simply stare at the closest wall. A voice murmured deep inside one of the cubicles, but it was nothing compared to the waves of sound that rose up during a typical morning.

She walked to where Wanda sat. Normally, the assistant would have put aside any pretense by the end of the day, and a trashy fan magazine would lie open on her keyboard. But no, the keyboard was bare as Wanda stared at her computer, so engrossed in whatever she was reading she didn't flinch when Rhetta approached.

The monitor had been cleared of the fluffy headed trolls, on Arianna's orders, but no one could squelch Wanda's individuality completely, and a tiny paper umbrella perched there jauntily. "Hey." Wanda didn't respond, at least not right away.

Finally, her assistant glanced up. "Spell exemplary," Wanda commanded, in lieu of a greeting.

"Say please," Rhetta teased, as she drew closer. Sometime during the day Wanda must have spritzed on more perfume, because the air around them smelled like sweet jasmine. Two pages of type lay side by side on Wanda's computer screen, but the images were miniscule. "You've got to be kidding. You can actually read that?"

Wanda swiveled, and then pointed at the reading glasses she wore. "Yeah, with these."

The glasses were a new touch, maybe to burnish her image in Arianna's eyes. The black frames made Wanda look like one of the oncology researchers in the lab downstairs. "Great frames, Wanda. How did you spell it?"

She shook her head. "I didn't write it. It's for the hospital's annual report."

"Annual report?" As a nonprofit, St. James Medical Center didn't do things like annual reports, or quarterly earnings statements, or stockholder meetings. It wasn't necessary, and it would have tarnished the hospital's reputation for serving the poor and uninsured. No, the hospital would never generate probing business stories in the *Los Angeles Examiner,* even though it was one of the area's largest employers and generated millions of dollars in revenue every year.

"They just call it an 'annual report' to make it sound official." Wanda had returned her attention to the computer screen, and with one keystroke, the image there morphed into a single frame. "I told them I'd read it before it went to press."

That made perfect sense. People asked the public relations staff to proof everything from employment ads to cafeteria menus to a thousand and one other things that had nothing at all to do with PR. It was a matter of goodwill that they always said yes, plus it was a good way to stay on top of the comings and goings at the hospital. "It's spelled right," Rhetta said, after a quick perusal. "Who does this go to?"

"Oh, you know, people who donate. Or people they wish would donate." Wanda pecked at her computer, and a different page popped up. Name after name scrolled down the screen, all of the names alphabetized in huge, block letters. "They had to supersize it," she explained, though Rhetta had yet to ask. "People kept saying they couldn't read their own name." She paused, and then glanced at Rhetta. "Are you on it?"

She hadn't even thought to check. The human resources rep had given her a thick stack of forms to sign at her orientation, but she didn't remember ever signing a donor card. By now that piece of paper probably lay forgotten at the bottom of her desk drawer. "No, I haven't signed up yet."

Wanda grunted, and then leaned back in her chair, clearly tired of staring at pages of type. "Your hunky friend's on the list." Wanda pointed at the screen with her index finger. "Says he's a major donor."

Rhetta cocked her head. "My friend?" She leaned over Wanda's shoulder again.

"Look." Wanda tapped the glass, ruffling the image. "Says Dr. Eamon McAllister gave more than ten thousand dollars last year. Impressive." Wanda nodded her head knowingly. "That'll take a bite out of your paycheck."

Right there, centered on the computer screen, was Eamon's name, second from the last, in a section reserved for "gold members." Unlike the lesser elements of silver and platinum, the gold members' names were printed in boldface.

"Well, what do you know." Turns out the good doctor was both handsome and generous. A very attractive combination in a man.

"I think it's great," Wanda said. "The hospital needs more people like him."

"You're right." The murmuring behind the cubicle wall had stopped, and it seemed they were the only two people left in the office. Funny how she had never thought a medical resident could afford a donation like that. A first-year resident, no less. "Let's call it quits, Wanda. We've all had enough excitement for one day."

And with that, Wanda turned off the computer program with a click.

Rhetta drove south through fading sun to the crowded streets of the shore after first bidding Wanda goodnight. Usually, the evening commute took her no more than ten minutes, unless she got stuck behind a rumbling *taqueria* truck, which might add another minute or two.

The short commute was a definite plus. She had suffered through four years of Los Angeles's freeways as an undergrad, which was long enough. Didn't matter if she was driving at two o'clock in the afternoon or at midnight, something was always breaking down or smashing up or falling over on the local freeway.

The best part of the drive now was when the skyscrapers of downtown Long Beach receded from her rearview mirror. She would open a window then and breathe in saltwater and seaweed, her hair whipping around her face. Her apartment was only five blocks from the beach, which she had counted out carefully before signing a rental agreement, and even hopped joyfully over cracks in the sidewalk on her way to the front door like a kid playing hopscotch.

She loved the shore, lined with its red-tiled roofs and sun-baked lawns. Of course, the houses were pressed so closely together neighbors often yelled to each other without cracking open a window, and an empty parking space was the most precious real estate of all, but that just added to the place's charm.

Luckily, there were no *taquería* trucks out today, and she sailed past stucco buildings. At the final intersection, she waited for a teenage boy with a boogie board to amble through the crosswalk. All tanned arms and legs, the boy had the dreamy smile of someone just back from the beach and he even walked differently . . . swaying from side to side like an ocean current. Like he was king of the world, and the road-weary commuters had no choice but to wait for him.

The fuzzy smile reminded her of someone else. She could imagine Nick like that—the saunter and flip-flops, a golden tan. But the stranger in front of her radiated good health, while her favorite beachcomber lay trapped by boxy equipment and impersonal faces back at the medical center. She frowned as the stranger sauntered along. How she wished she could have taken Nick's place. She would happily trade places with him so that he could watch the bodysurfer, while she would lie in ICU, where day and night merged and sun never cracked the surface.

She feebly waved, and drove through the intersection instead of turning right. The street was broad and clean, and queen

66

palm trees swayed overhead. She was on the main boulevard now . . . a conflux of funky bead shops, knickknack stores, and vintage clothiers, sitting side by side with a bland bank storefront and the ever-present coffee bar. Some of the mom-and-pop stores had been there for years, she could tell, and they resolutely refused to budge for newcomers. She had all the time in the world to ponder this because cars couldn't move more than twenty miles an hour here. Once in a while, a sports car might try to break away from the pack and sail down the boulevard, but the crush of cars and buses would always keep it in check.

Finally she arrived at the bridge and turned onto the main beach highway. Already the air felt cooler now, as she drove along a less congested stretch of road that would take her to the surf.

She knew where she had to go. She could push most of her fears for Nick to the recesses of her mind while she was at work. But here, away from it all, the sight of a bodysurfer had brought them forward again. She drove until she reached the beach parking lot and pulled into an empty space by a cinder-block wall. The wind swirled around her as she stepped from her car, gritty puffs of sand prickling her ankles.

The object of her desire, and the thing that had taken her two miles off course, sat to the west. The old pier was made entirely of wood slats worn thin by a century of ocean swells. At the base of the pier sat a bronze sculpture of a seal, so pretty in the fading light. Most people paid no mind to the statue in their hurry to reach the sand.

But unlike them, Rhetta understood the sculpture was one of the best parts of the pier. It brought good luck, said the surfers who plied the ocean swells. It had been there forever, long before the diner at the end of the pier, or the bait shop next to it. While she didn't have anything nearly as dangerous in mind as the surfers, she wasn't above a little superstition, so she walked to the sculpture, closed her eyes, and lifted her palm to the bronze animal's nose. Twice, she rubbed it.

The metal was shiny from use, and surprisingly warm. She withdrew her hand and blinked. It was such a silly tradition; one that probably wouldn't make any difference to Nick. But then again, he needed all of the luck he could get. She stepped away from the sculpture, half-expecting it to repay her faith with a wink. But the seal's gaze remained trained on the horizon beyond, as if the bronze animal was searching for something just beyond its grasp.

Her pilgrimage complete, Rhetta slowly returned to her car and drove back the way she had come, taking the coast highway to the boulevard, and then driving into the shores. The traffic was as thick as ever, and it took her a good twenty minutes to arrive at her doorstep. Once there, the two-story apartment building began to gradually cheer her. With its graceful curved doorways, sunbaked tile roof, and shock of magenta bougainvillea that climbed the east wall, it looked as if it had always been on this corner and always would, no matter what happened with the rest of the neighborhood.

She parked her car and made her way up the walk, where she bent to retrieve the *Los Angeles Examiner* from her doormat, and slide her key into the iron lock. The heavy door swung open to reveal gleaming hardwood floors and a two-story ceiling that towered overhead. For some reason, she always felt like yelling that she was home, though there would be no one to hear her. *No matter.* She kicked off her heels and plopped onto a twill couch in front of the fireplace with the newspaper. *First things first.* She skipped the front section of the *Examiner*, letting it slide to the floor, and began to read the local news. While most people could peruse the paper at their leisure—maybe after watching television or having a second cup of coffee—she accepted the nightly ritual as part of her work. She dutifully read about the latest controversies with the local city council, the water department, and the transportation agency, one eye ever-vigilant for any mention at all of St. James Medical Center.

Everything else could wait, including her own supper, while she read the articles and bylines. She had just turned to the last page of the local section when a story about the police department stopped her short. The article didn't include a picture, but the words stood out as clearly as if they had been printed in all capital letters. Seems there was an investigation underway in the police department. An undercover investigation by internal affairs to catch officers suspected of inflating their timesheets. The story mentioned that one of the men, in particular, had pulled down one hundred fifty thousand dollars in overtime the year before, while his immediate supervisor had earned only half as much. The story was only mildly interesting to her—with a force of more than nine thousand cops, something was always happening with the local police department—until one particular name caught her attention. The story explained that five officers were under investigation, including one Officer Larry Belknap, a twenty-year veteran with the force.

That couldn't be right. She read the paragraph once, twice, then three times. Her stomach growled angrily on the third reading, but dinner would just have to wait. Officer Larry Belknap. All of those telephone messages. Why would Larry track her down to find out about Nick's condition, when he could have called Beryl just as easily?

She laid the newspaper in her lap. He seemed intensely curious about her visit to the ICU. Too curious. Something about this didn't sit right. And what was worse . . . she had a sneaking suspicion that whatever it was, it didn't bode well for Nick, either.

CHAPTER 7

Dr. Eamon McAllister already was in room 715 when Rhetta arrived the next morning, Tuesday. He stared at a computer screen next to Nick's bed, so enthralled with whatever he was reading, he didn't seem to notice she'd walked right up behind him.

"Hi, Eamon." She smiled and reached out to flatten a hill of sheet that bunched around Nick's chest. The sweetheart was fast asleep. The crinkled plastic tube had been re-taped to his throat with what looked like white packaging tape. "How's our patient doing today?"

"Worse than yesterday." Eamon barely glanced up; he seemed to be memorizing whatever was on the screen in front of him. "His glands are swollen, his lung capacity's down. There's no way we can take the tube out until his lungs get stronger. His vitals don't look good."

Rhetta winced. A doctor like Eamon could be blunt, because he was trained to look at a heart, an arm, a lung, and see only tissue and veins. It must be nice to be able to dissect an illness—to pull it apart at its roots and inspect it from the inside out, piece by piece—instead of seeing one whole. Instead of seeing Nick.

"What about Siegel—isn't he Nick's internist?" she asked. "Can't he do anything?" St. James was supposed to be one of the finest hospitals this side of Los Angeles, for goodness sake. Every year, a busload of medical residents showed up in the lobby, creases on their lab coats needle-sharp, faces scrubbed, with newly purchased stethoscopes glinting against their chests, all shapes and sizes, all ears, hoping to learn from the greatest minds in medicine; only the greatest minds in medicine hadn't a clue how to help Nick right now, dammit. Sometimes, the more she knew about medicine, the more she didn't want to know.

"You're not going to let him die, are you?" she softly said.

"We've got to reverse the symptoms. There's always a specialty hospital in Phoenix, but that's worse-case scenario. He's only been here a few days, you know."

That was scant comfort. The longer a patient stayed in ICU, the more likely he would never get out; she knew that. If the original diagnosis didn't kill him, an infection, or having to rely on a man-made machine to pump his blood and breathe his air, would.

"How did you say you knew Nick?" Eamon cocked his head at her.

She hadn't realized she was holding Nick's hand, and she released it. "College. Remember? We were together once, but I couldn't go through with it."

The doctor studied her. "Interesting. Why don't we grab some coffee and you can tell me all about it?"

"I guess I have a few minutes." Reluctantly she glanced away from Nick. He would never know if she left for a moment or two. "I can't stay long, though."

The doctor offered her his arm, and they walked through the double-wide door, which was just the right size for a surgical bed or a wheelchair to pass through. It seemed surreal, but not uncomfortable, to be walking alongside Dr. Eamon McAllister, with their elbows touching, past closed doors, through patches of shade and then light, as the glow from one fluorescent bulb evaporated before another one could begin.

Even though it was morning—a bright, beautiful June morning from what she could tell when she'd walked from the employee parking lot into the hospital—here every light had been dimmed. When an orderly came toward them, wheeling a large linen bag with towels and sheets, he seemed to be moving in slow motion. How disorienting for patients' families to visit a place where day and night merged, where one day flowed into the next and all that changed were the faces of the orderlies and the nurses.

Before the end of the hall, before they reached a door that opened out onto the lobby and the real world, Eamon stopped in front of a sterile, laminate-topped kitchenette. There was a huge coffeepot, a jar of creamer, and a tower of plastic cups, but nothing else. He withdrew the coffeepot and two cups, swirled the remains around once or twice, and then poured out liquid. There was hardly any steam—it was too late in the morning for that—and even the smell had dissipated. He held onto both cups as he ushered her through the final door and into the lobby. But he didn't turn left, like she thought he would. He turned right, where the only thing on the blank wall was the transom of an unmarked door.

He handed her one of the cups, which was pointless really, since she had no intention of drinking stale coffee, and then swung open the door. An inch of baby-blue sky peeked around the door's edge, then another, as he pushed it further. A warm breeze blew through the crack and tickled her cheek. The unfiltered air felt so good against her chilled skin. She stepped cautiously over the threshold, where her heel landed on a tarpaper roof that scratched like sandpaper.

It was a beautiful morning, after all . . . just as she'd thought. The sky was a clear aqua, a reflection of the Pacific Ocean, and a thin net of clouds stretched from end to end. A waist-high concrete wall ringed the roof and forced the breeze to roll upward, until it swirled around her stomach and chest.

Without a second thought, she laid the coffee cup on tarpaper and dashed to the far southern corner. She leaned over the metal flashing as far as she could and saw tiny matchbox-sized cars zigzag across the hospital's parking lot. Beyond that, a longer line of cars caravanned down the main boulevard.

"Hey, not so fast," Eamon called as he ran up behind her. "Do you want to be the first person to lose her life up here?"

Laughing, she took in the panorama before her. An insurance building looked like a shiny Rubik's Cube across the way, its mirrored squares clicked into place. People were probably going about their business inside, answering telephones, eating at their desks, and maybe even watching them, too. "How did you know you could get up here?"

He shrugged. "Dumb luck. I come up here between surgeries sometimes." He reached behind him, where an air-conditioning vent sprouted like a silver mushroom planted in dirt, and withdrew two folded beach chairs hidden behind it. With a snap, he opened one chair, then the other, and set them both down. "Here you go." He motioned to the empty chair.

"Thanks." She carefully sat down, smoothing the chiffon skirt under her thighs; a flimsy barrier between her skin and the prickly plastic webbing. Sunlight warmed her face; it reminded her of the seascape back in her office. The tiles of speckled tarpaper, cresting at the seams? They looked like acres of black sand, dimpled into miniature mountains by an ocean breeze. The droning air conditioner with the mechanical cadence that rose and fell on each revolution? It could have been the engines of a cruise boat, way out in the distance . . . maybe an ocean liner on a five-day trip to Mexico. Warmth penetrated her skin down to her sore muscles, to her stiff back. She'd been working so hard, worrying so much over the past few days, that last night, as she was brushing her teeth back in her apartment, she had spied dark rings under her almond eyes. *Well, that was a first.* She'd even slipped a tube of concealer into her purse as she left her apartment building. But here, now, everything was warming, and she slumped against the beach chair.

"I need to tell you something about Nick." Eamon's voice brought her back to the hospital, to the rooftop, to the floor below them, to Nick lying so still in the semi-dark. "Siegel thinks he has a diagnosis."

She opened her eyes. They were definitely back on the rooftop.

"It looks like Nick has respiratory distress syndrome." Eamon squinted at her. "Basically, his lungs are attacking his body."

"I don't understand."

He reached over and took her hand, still squinting. "It's not over, Rhetta. There's an experimental drug we could try that uses medicine and an oxygen chamber. It's a start, and I've seen it work with other patients."

"Tell me the truth. Do you think he's going to make it?" He seemed so cool, so clinical.

"A lot of experimental procedures work. It could work with Nick."

"Well, it's got to work, that's all." Her tone sounded harsh now. While she knew he wasn't to blame, he'd been the one to deliver the bad news, after all. "You know, Nick's only thirty."

"Look, we just got the diagnosis. Don't jump the gun, okay?" He draped his arm around her shoulders protectively. "If it makes you feel better, I'll talk to the pulmonologist. We'll know what's up in a day or two."

She could have folded her arms and dropped her head onto her lap right then and there and stayed inert for hours or even days. But the sound of waves was too faint now. Try as she might, she couldn't conjure up the crash of saltwater, the blast from a cruise boat horn in the distance, or the sweet rest of melting under warm sunshine.

"I know," he said. "Have dinner with me tonight. We can talk about it."

She smiled wanly. "That won't help Nick much, will it?"

"No, but it'll make you feel better."

Maybe he was right. Maybe a good meal was what she needed, after all. A chance to sort this out, away from the hospital, away from her office and away from Nick, even.

"Seven o'clock," he said, before she had a chance to respond. "I'll pick you up." He withdrew his arm from around her shoulder. "And I don't take no for an answer."

It was only Tuesday, which was not the best time for a date. It was a school night, her grandmother would have said if she was visiting with her on the deck, but it didn't really matter. "Okay. Seven o'clock. I've got to get back to work now."

"I'll call you. Don't forget."

Slowly, she rose from the chair. "I won't forget. See you tonight." She walked toward the door in even, measured steps. She didn't exhale until she stood back in the hallway, outside the ICU, once more in semi-darkness and chilled air.

Confidence . . . she liked that in a man. Too much? Maybe, but at least he knew what he wanted. Time would tell if he would call her, or if he would blow the whole thing off. That didn't happen very often—she was usually the one to beg off dates with a cold, or some phony commitment she happened to remember at the last minute, or maybe a "surprise" visit from an old friend—anything to get away from those pesky EMS guys. But, just the same, it did happen.

And nothing would change with Nick over the course of one dinner. He would still be lying in the ICU, fitfully asleep, tethered to the respirator. Nothing she did would change that overnight.

★ ★ ★ ★ ★

As soon as she exited the elevator, Rhetta stepped into the hospital's lobby. The first person she happened to see was Beryl, who stood across the way. The woman looked utterly exhausted. Even though she wore a fuchsia smock today, crisscrossed with colorful streaks, her face looked pale and drawn, and deep rings circled her eyes.

"Beryl," she called out.

"Hey, Rhetta." Beryl sounded as tired as she looked. Her feet shuffled along the carpet as she moved to where Rhetta stood. "How are you doing?"

"A better question is . . . how are you doing?"

"Hanging in there," Beryl said. "Do you have a second?"

It was getting late; she would be missed back at the office. By now Arianna could be searching for her, and she wasn't in the mood to hear her name broadcast over the hospital's intercom. But she sensed that Beryl needed to talk. "I guess so."

She retreated a few steps into the lobby, pulled out a chair, and sat down, resting her elbows on her knees. She still couldn't get over how tired Beryl looked.

"Nick's not back from his tests yet and I could sure use some company."

"No problem."

Beryl chose to sit in a chair across from her. Noonday sun flowed through the lobby, highlighting every corner. Instead of speaking, Beryl toyed with a delicate gold chain that looped her neck, centered by a diamond pendant forged into a heart. Every so often, a ray of light illuminated the pendant like a glowing ember. Rhetta glanced at it again. The heart wasn't one solid diamond, after all. It was a cluster of stones that only gave the illusion of being whole. So delicate and light.

"Love the necklace. Is it new?" she asked.

"What. This? No, Nick gave it to me a few years ago." Beryl

76

held the necklace away from her throat to give Rhetta a better view.

Somehow, Rhetta couldn't picture Nick standing in front of a counter at the jewelry store, his blue uniform an inky blot against the shiny glass. The way he must have fingered the delicate chain in his beefy hands. "You're kidding, right?"

Beryl arched an eyebrow. "It was a guilt gift." She let the pendant fall back against her throat, where it glimmered like a sequined button.

"A guilt gift?"

"It's a long story. Do you really want to hear about it?"

No, what she really wanted to do was to leave the lobby and return to her office before Arianna could discover she was gone. But what choice did she have? "I guess."

Beryl studied the carpet first, before speaking. "A few years ago I was working a lot of overtime. We got seventy bucks an hour for the night shift. Since Nick was on patrol, I thought it didn't matter if I was gone all night." She glanced up. "Only one time he wasn't expecting me to come home."

The story had appeared out of nowhere. She'd expected Beryl to tell her something silly about how Nick had come to purchase such a dainty necklace for his wife. She didn't want to hear this, especially since Nick lay in a hospital bed above them suffering through yet another test. So she averted her eyes, and pretended to study the wall, the elevator door, the ceiling tiles. While she couldn't stop Beryl from telling her the sordid details of their marriage, she didn't have to encourage her, either.

"Anyway, I came home early one time. There was a strange car at our curb, but I thought maybe one of my neighbors had a friend over."

Beryl continued to toy with the necklace, which twinkled with reflected light. "The girl was young, Rhetta. Really young. She was standing in front of my refrigerator and I went ballistic.

I called her every name in the book. But then Nick walked in and told me it wasn't like that."

Beryl's voice had risen, and the pendant danced with each word. "He said she was a rookie, having dinner. My leftovers."

It seemed only right to defend Nick, given everything that had gone on. "You believed him, didn't you?" Rhetta asked.

"Yeah, but I checked the bed first. There was nothing. It was all made up like I left it. So he got off the hook. And I got a necklace." She smiled sadly. "I guess everything turned out okay."

Poor Beryl. She'd come home from a long night's work only to find a strange woman in her kitchen. While she didn't think Nick would ever cheat on his wife like that, she had to admire Beryl's restraint. If it was her, she might have coldcocked Nick right then and there. Acted first and asked questions later. But that was her.

"Course, divorce was never an option," Beryl said. "Nick told me on the day we got married we were stuck with each other. Said he'd never divorce me . . . ever. Didn't believe in it, being Catholic and all. Said if I wanted to leave him, I'd better come up with something permanent."

The last few words hung awkwardly in the air, but Beryl didn't seem to notice.

"So that's my story."

Not knowing what to say, Rhetta began to rise to her feet. It was only a matter of time before Arianna would figure out that she wasn't in her office. "I'm sorry, Beryl. Sorry you had to go through all that. And that Nick's not doing any better. But I'm afraid I have to get back to work. Call me if they find out anything with the tests. *Anything.* Or if you need to talk. And take care of yourself, okay?"

Beryl nodded, absentmindedly. The last thing Rhetta noticed as she walked away from the lobby was the way that Beryl held the necklace between her thumb and forefinger. The skin on her fingertips had slowly turned to white.

Chapter 8

After speaking with Beryl, Rhetta retreated to her office, mulling the nurse's words as she walked. When she approached the door to her office, she spied a memo taped to the doorjamb, with Arianna's initials sprawled across one corner.

At least the message was short: media conference @ two. Rhetta glanced down at her watch and yelped. She'd have to run if she wanted to make it to the press conference on time. Nothing like running from one troubling situation to another.

"Hold my calls," she said to Wanda, as she rounded her assistant's desk. This week Wanda was reading a torrid romance novel set in South America, and she barely looked up as Rhetta sped by. "Hold my calls, okay?" Rhetta repeated, one foot already in the hall. When Wanda finally nodded, Rhetta dashed down the corridor, cursed the heaving elevators, and opted instead for the stairwell. She arrived at the press conference, panting, just as a security guard shut the heavy metal doors to the auditorium.

Around her, a handful of people sat in cloth-backed chairs that ringed a podium, and a few scraggly types fidgeted with skinny, celadon green notebooks. It was quite a turnout for Dr. Visser's latest appearance before the media. This conference offered him the chance to deny once and for all that he had used drugs the morning he operated on the city councilman.

The people around her looked like newspaper reporters and were probably from the local papers. One woman, who sat in the first row, wore a tan blazer and tennis shoes, and her bangs slanted, as if she had cut them herself. No two reporters sat together, Rhetta noticed, almost as if there was an unspoken code that each person should get his own private space. She broke the code by sitting next to the woman with the crooked bangs.

In front of her, a group of radio reporters jostled around a wooden podium in the middle of the stage, trying to attach shiny microphones to the hospital's lone, old-fashioned one. The microphones were boxed in by call letters from the stations—KTRT, KMX, KPCC. The smaller the station, the bigger the call letters were printed, or so it seemed.

Behind the radio reporters, a trio of dark-suited men huddled together. *Ah, the legal team.* She had heard Arianna say the hospital's lawyers had urged her to cancel the press conference. When Dr. Visser would have none of that, they insisted they be included in the front row, to stop the proceedings if need be. Normally harried and rumpled, dressed in rolled-up shirtsleeves and permanent frowns, today the attorneys looked spit-and-polished in charcoal pinstriped suits and crisp oxford shirts. However, the frowns remained.

She turned around after studying the men. Only two television reporters had arrived. Lisa Simmons, the blond bombshell from Channel 7, flirted with a bearded cameraman at the back of the auditorium, while Dallas George from Channel 5 stood next to her with his back to the chairs, practicing a "cut-in" that would later appear on the nightly news.

Unlike the ragtag print reporters who exchanged bored looks, Dallas wore an impeccably tailored olive green suit, a beige foulard tie, and a perfectly folded satin pocket square. He didn't seem particularly good-looking this close up; he was older than Rhetta remembered. Thick lines framed his mouth and eyes, as if years of wearing pancake makeup had made the stuff seep into his skin. The two television reporters ignored each other as they smoothed down their hair and adjusted their jackets.

After a moment, Arianna waltzed down the center aisle. She wore a crimson suit with oversized buttons and matching red lipstick. Perfect for the camera, but then again, her boss already knew that.

The suit was skintight, of course, and it forced Arianna to inch along in baby steps toward the stage. When she arrived, she ducked behind a heavy velvet curtain and reemerged with Dr. Visser, who looked completely at ease behind the podium they had set up . . . jocular, even. If he was at all concerned about the proceedings, one couldn't tell. He even held a laminated picture of the human body that had clear sheets layered on top of each other, like the pull-out charts she would giggle over as a little girl while reading the encyclopedia section on the male anatomy.

Her boss leaned into the microphone. "Thank y'all for coming today," she said sweetly, her eyes raking the auditorium. "As y'all know, here at St. James we believe in honesty and integrity, and we're not afraid to answer your questions." She turned to gaze at Dr. Visser. One second, two seconds, three seconds.

Nice touch, Rhetta thought.

"You may have heard about an unfortunate incident. Something occurred during Councilman Griago's operation, which Dr. Visser can explain."

Arianna waved her hand back with a flourish to indicate the doctor. "For those of you who don't know our distinguished surgeon, may I introduce Dr. Jeremy Visser."

A light clicked on, coming from somewhere in the back of the room, and a bright circle zeroed in on Dr. Visser. It meant Arianna's sound bite hadn't been filmed after all, so it wouldn't be on the nightly news. Rhetta knew her boss would be angry about that.

"Well now, I think we all know why we're here." The physician grinned wryly. "Recent medical research indicates that kidney removal does not contraindicate good health." As he spoke, he propped the chart against the podium and the reporters scribbled furiously, though she noticed he hadn't said anything meaningful yet.

He continued to speak in a breezy, confident tone, as if he were addressing a class of first-year medical residents. As if he actually enjoyed the proceedings. "Once we had the patient under general anesthesia, I employed a transperitoneal subcostal incision." At this, the doctor ran his finger along the top layer of the chart, which showed a human stomach drawn in peach and red. "Because of the patient's advanced age"—the councilman was only forty-five, or about the same age as Dr. Visser—"I opted for an open procedure, instead of a laparoscopy. You'll note from the chart that views of the kidneys may be somewhat obstructed by the thoracic cage."

Although her understanding of medicine was rudimentary at best, Rhetta knew that the doctor was talking about the councilman's ribs.

Someone raised a hand behind her—causing a whoosh of air to tickle her neck—but the doctor continued. "My first objective was to oblate the ureter and blood vessels before removing the kidney." He drew back the first sheet, which revealed a diagram of blood vessels that traversed the human form. "Now, was there perirenal fascia?" He asked the question as if he fully expected the reporters, who looked dumbstruck, to answer him. She could tell they didn't understand a word he was saying. "I didn't suspect that, so I—"

The reporter next to Rhetta finally jumped to her feet. "That's all well and good, doctor," she said, jabbing her pencil in the air for emphasis, "but what does this mean for the patient? Will the councilman survive?"

The doctor's face hardened. "If you were listening at the beginning, my dear, you would have heard that subcutaneous removal of a kidney does not equate with certain morbidity." He returned his gaze to the chart at his side. "Now, as I was saying—"

"What about the nurse? She says there were drugs involved." Rhetta turned to see Dallas George step forward dramatically from the shadows, camera light illuminating the left side of his face. He had planted one foot squarely in front of the other, as if he was battling a mortal enemy. From beyond the brightness, the silhouette of Lisa Simmons also moved a tad closer to the stage.

"Sources say it's not the first time. And why hasn't the anesthesiologist come forward?" The newswoman glanced sideways before lowering her microphone, as if to gauge Dallas George's reaction.

Rhetta swirled around. The press conference was beginning to take on a life of its own.

So she half-rose, prepared to walk to the stage and explain, in her most official public relations voice, that the hospital had certain protocols for dealing with this type of incident and they would keep reporters up-to-date on the councilman's condition . . . blah, blah, blah. The words would roll off her tongue, after spending so many afternoons listening to Arianna go on and on in her best corporate-speak, and after dozens of public relations conferences. She knew the exact words to say, because she'd seen this game played out before. It wasn't about getting at the truth, it was about getting a juicy sound bite, and getting it first. A simple power play, with both reporters trying to outmaneuver the other, so that they could prove their worth. Self-serving and twisted, it happened all the time. But not here, not now.

The doctor beat her to it. Dropping the chart to the floor, Dr. Visser leaned forward and grasped the center microphone, which caused the radio reporters to wince behind their earpieces.

"This was a case of an anatomical obstruction, clear and simple," the doctor spat. "We'll begin the selection process post-haste to find a suitable kidney donor." He glared at the reporter in the front row. "However, since there seems to be a question about my mental state at the time, all I can do is refer you to medicine's most esteemed journal—*The Recorder*. That publication has named me its top surgeon this month. It doesn't matter what anyone else—including the anesthesiologist—has to say. Now if you'll excuse me, I'm needed back in surgery."

Rhetta glanced at her watch as she sat down again. It was already way past two o'clock, which was far too late for a surgery to start. The doctor was lying.

He glowered at the reporters as he stormed off the stage. He looked angry that he had been forced to answer their questions, when *he* was the one who had insisted on holding this press conference. He was the one who couldn't resist the chance to be quoted, again, even under suspect circumstances.

But maybe that famous circus showman was right; maybe there was no such thing as bad publicity. Guaranteed, the reporters would be calling Dr. Visser again as soon as they needed another quote in a hurry. Or, as *he* would say, post-haste. And the doctor would be more than willing to indulge them.

She also knew, as clearly as she knew her own name, that she would be summoned to Arianna's office after all of this to explain why she hadn't done anything to stop the circus. Why hadn't she saved Dr. Visser from himself? Rhetta had known the words to say, but she couldn't force them out fast enough. She promised herself right then and there she wouldn't make that mistake again.

CHAPTER 9

The searing pain subsided in Nick's abdomen as he lay in room 715 of the intensive care unit. He overhead a voice whisper "code blue" from somewhere far above him, but it didn't matter. Long-forgotten memories had seeped to the forefront now, and pushed away all physical sensations . . . all other sights and sounds. The end had come, and he took a final breath.

Chapter 10

As evening approached, after the reporters and cameramen and attorneys went away, Rhetta drove back to her apartment. She stood in front of an oval mirror in her bedroom for a long time, watching her reflection critically as she quarter-turned. She'd hurriedly changed into a cream-colored pantsuit for her dinner with Eamon, which was a little slinky, maybe, what with the rayon and all, but she was too tired to riffle through her closet once again.

She tried to muster a smile. For the past few days she'd been so worried about Nick, so troubled by questions over his diagnosis, that she didn't have time to think about much else. She probably would have said no to the doctor's invitation, but then he'd smiled, and out came those brilliant white teeth again. Maybe if he wasn't so charming, so good-looking, she would have stayed home tonight and curled up on the couch with the *Los Angeles Examiner* instead of going heaven-only-knew where for dinner with him.

As an afterthought, she snatched a favorite scarf from the vanity and knotted it around her neck. She rarely used it—an elegant print on silk—because it was so expensive. But when she took the job at St. James and moved into this apartment, her grandmother wrote to say that every girl needed one treasured scarf, and she enclosed the money for this one. No, the clothes looked perfect; that wasn't it. Leaning forward, she rubbed her finger under her right eye, but the blue-black remained. The problem was that no amount of makeup was going to hide the fact that she hadn't slept well ever since Nick had been admitted and Dr. Visser had gone off the deep end.

But still . . . she placed her hands on her hips and smiled. It was an old trick from junior high, when she pretended to be a supermodel on a photo shoot for a teen magazine, who posed for a photographer who was standing somewhere behind the mirror. An exotic Frenchman perhaps, named Jacque or Henri. It always boosted her confidence to think of a photographer taking her picture, asking her to turn this way and that. She'd click her tongue against the roof of her mouth and hear the shutter of a camera. Smile, click. Smile, click. Turn, click. It seemed to work when she was in junior high, but now she felt silly.

So she grabbed a pair of ivory pumps, and tiptoed from the room. She always waited until the very last minute to put on her heels to keep them from scratching the beautiful mahogany floors. The wooden planks were one reason she took the apartment in the first place—not to mention a carved plaster archway that separated the living room from the entry. If she closed her eyes and opened them again, real fast, she could pretend she was in a Moorish castle with curves and whitewashed walls and wide-plank floors. Never mind that traffic honked by at all hours of the day and night, and a milk truck stopped at a corner grocery at four o'clock in the morning, Saturdays included, with a cheerful blast of its horn.

As if on cue, the front doorbell rang, a sound as deep and resonant as a church bell. She paused before opening the heavy Spanish door. Rising on tiptoe, she peered through a dime-sized peephole and saw Eamon, who was carefully studying his shoes on the cracked concrete landing with a bunch of plum tulips peeking out from behind his back. He'd slicked down his hair tonight and even the wayward curl lay flat and shiny against his neck. He wore a double-breasted tan suit, which made him look completely different. Not better, or worse . . . just different.

After a second he looked up at her, or up at the peephole, and she pulled back in surprise.

"Hi," she said, as she tugged open the heavy door.

"Hello." He withdrew his arm and produced the tulips, which were bound with a silk bow. "I thought you might like these." He handed her the bouquet.

"They're beautiful." The bulbs were so heavy they drooped over the plastic sheath. She stared at them longer than she intended, but she couldn't think of a single thing to say. "Come on in. I'll get water for these."

When he walked in, she smelled fresh soap and mint toothpaste. His shoulders looked broader and his eyes bluer than before.

"I thought I'd take you somewhere different tonight. Somewhere you've never been."

She laughed. "Well, haven't you done that before? Besides, it shouldn't be too hard. What with work and all, I don't get out much." She gripped the bouquet awkwardly—the stems were threatening to drip water all over the beautiful mahogany floor. "C'mon."

She walked through the living room and into the kitchen, where a row of boxy glass cabinets lined the walls. Under the cabinets squatted an ancient Viking stove, painted cherry red and with dozens of hairline cracks that swirled around the burners. Black and white checkered linoleum tiles covered the floor beneath it. "Vintage kitchen!" the apartment's ad had bragged. "Cook's delight!" Adding whole milk to a box of macaroni and cheese was about the closest she had ever come to cooking anything, but the ad had made everything sound so good. And who knew . . . maybe macaroni and cheese did taste better when it was warmed up on the quaint stove.

She opened a cabinet, slid aside some wine goblets and plastic tumblers, and then spied a mason jar hiding in a corner. It would do nicely. "Thank you for the flowers," she said, as she turned to face him. "They really are gorgeous."

"My pleasure." He leaned casually against the kitchen island. "I like the apartment. It suits you."

"Thanks." She peeled off the plastic sheath and gripped the stems tightly. *Was she supposed to cut off one inch or two?* "It's a little close to downtown." She should make one-inch cuts, definitely. She laid the stems on the cutting board and sliced them horizontally with a steak knife.

"Oh, I don't know. There's always the theatre, and some pretty great restaurants. You have to give it a chance."

"You have a good attitude, Doctor. I'm sure your patients appreciate that." She gathered up the flowers, and then held the mason jar under the tap until water filled it halfway, self-conscious under his gaze.

"Everything's a matter of perspective. Beside, don't you know it's a big, blank slate when you're in California? Anything's possible." He stood behind her now. She definitely smelled fresh soap with a chaser of mint mouthwash.

"I suppose. Okay, I'm ready to go. Let me grab something." She had tossed a blue-jean jacket onto the oversized couch in the middle of the living room, which was a relic from her college days. "All set." They walked past the plaster fireplace, then around the couch. Her cell phone lay between two of the fat cushions and she scooped it up and dropped it lightly into the jacket's pocket.

Gallantly, he opened the front door for her. A gray convertible hugged the curb, freshly washed. It was the same car she'd seen in the doctor's parking lot. "Nice ride, Doctor. Typical, but nice." Too bad it wasn't the lime green electric car; now *that* would have made him even more interesting.

He chuckled. "You don't get out much, huh? I wonder why."

She settled into the sports car, smiling, and he closed the door. The cushions curved around and enveloped her, like a cockpit must envelop the pilot of a 747. Only this cockpit had burled wood and an expensive surround-sound stereo. He slid into the driver's seat and patted her knee when they turned onto the main highway. They didn't speak, but with warm air blowing through the car it would have been hard to hear anything, anyway. The sports car zigged and zagged through the neon signs of downtown Long Beach, until, finally, a highway billboard announced their arrival at a beach up north, about thirty minutes later. He maneuvered the car onto a side street, and then into a freshly painted parking garage.

They now faced a weathered pier. The pier's squat corners reached out into the Pacific Ocean like broken points on a starfish. She'd seen the old pier on the Channel 11 news, when it had almost burned down shortly after she arrived at the medical center. An East Coast syndicate had worked around the clock since then to restore the pier's planks. The news report showed film footage of newly arrived immigrants fishing for grouper off its side, while trendy clubsters sauntered by, headed for Club Moxie, each with something entirely different in mind. She had also learned that, come about midnight, local gang-bangers swaggered down the pier so most families left the area long before that.

Eamon parked, crossed in front of the sports car, then took her hand and helped her rise from the seat. Instead of bounding up the concrete steps, into the glow of Craig's Hot Dog on a Stick, he pointed out a line of boats that stood at attention in the harbor. Sleek sailboats, their masts jutting high into the night, sat side by side, gently lolling, their tethers creaking with each swell in the water. They sounded eerily like ghosts rattling chains on a haunted pirate ship.

She scooped up the blue-jean jacket before leaving the car. The air felt warm, humid, just right for June. They walked beside an iron fence that separated them from the yachts, and when they reached a certain gate, Eamon took a key from the same ring as his convertible's, opened the lock, and gestured toward a boat slip. The smell of motor oil wafted over the air, and a thin film of it coated the water. She could also smell brine and some linseed oil that the deckhands must have used to polish all of that teak.

"I thought we'd eat at my place." He pointed to an ebony sailboat, the tallest one in the bunch. A web of ropes and pulleys, improbably knotted, soared above their heads like rigging in a circus tent. He hopped onto the deck, then wrapped his arms around her waist, scooped her up, and deposited her next to him.

"Wait a second." She reached down to slide off her pumps, but the boat careened lazily to the left and she nearly fell out of his arms and onto the deck. She grabbed for his hand at the last minute.

"It's okay." He grinned down at her. "After a while you won't even feel it."

Clumsily, she released his hand, and then followed him down a few stairs, into a dimly lit cabin. Some art deco chairs, clustered in groups of twos and threes, surrounded cocktail tables, each of which held a thickly cut crystal lamp that glowed in the half-light. Everything was so beautiful. Glancing up, she faced her own reflection, splintered and glimmering, in hundreds of mirrored tiles that swirled around the ceiling. The roof looked exactly like a giant disco ball that had been squashed flat. It reminded her of a lounge in an ocean liner, circa 1920, and all that was missing was a flapper doing the Lindy front and center of the sleek room.

She blinked when he switched on the lights. The room was

pure white. From pleated curtains that flowed down from the ceiling, to plump cushions on a low couch that hugged the opposite wall, it was all stunningly, beautifully white. Like a snowstorm. Like heaven, probably. "And they say medical residents are poor." The table lamps definitely were French crystal, too. "Seems to me medicine already has been very good to you."

He moved behind a platinum-covered bar set against the back wall, and wordlessly reached for a martini glass that hung upside down. He tipped it toward her as a question.

"Sure." She ran her hand down a panel of well-oiled teak. "What's your secret? You're not running drugs down to Mexico with this thing, are you?"

He laughed and poured some vodka into a silver jigger, which had a curlicue monogram on its front, of course. "Let's say I found a creative way to finance medical school." He disappeared behind the bar for an instant, then reappeared with a vermouth bottle, which he tipped into the jigger. He swirled the drink around like a seasoned bartender before pouring it into a delicately stemmed martini glass and offering it to her. "And my way didn't involve any scholarships."

She took the drink warily. The picture was so perfect—the sailboat, the convertible, him—maybe she should change the subject, while she still had time. "You don't have to tell me about it, you know."

He grinned and returned to the bar. "Truth is, my way almost landed me in jail. Turns out med school students can get all the pot they want, but uppers are a different story." He stared at her hard, as if waiting for her reaction. "I'm pretty sure Nick knows I was dealing."

He'd have to wait a little longer. "What does Nick have to do with this?"

"I think he found out about it, that's all."

Eamon began to expertly mix himself a drink. The alabaster surroundings, the twinkling lights, the mirrored ceiling; all of it had taken on a hard edge and it began to look to her more like the ballroom of a gaudy hotel than heaven, now. "What happens if Nick gets back on the police force?" She quickly corrected herself, "I mean, *when* he gets back on the force." Finally, she took a sip of her martini, and felt the icy cold against her teeth.

"We'll see. I had him over for dinner a few nights before he was admitted. He didn't seem to think it was a big deal. At least, I hope not." Eamon shook his head. "My family couldn't afford community college, let alone medical school. Hell, fifty thousand dollars a year might as well have been fifty million as far as they were concerned."

Carefully, he ran his thumb over and around the edge of the martini glass, until the memory passed and his face relaxed. "Anyway, that was then. All that matters is that I made it through school and no one got hurt . . . not really." Now he seemed almost relieved, as if he'd practiced that small speech a million times until it all made sense to him. "C'mon. I'll show you the rest of the boat."

Reluctantly, Rhetta placed her drink on the bar and followed him across the cabin. So he wasn't perfect. Not even close. He was still so different from anyone she'd ever met. Most of the men she knew still scrounged around for happy hour buffets, looking for places to order a beer or two and a plate of nachos to make their paychecks stretch until Friday. But not Eamon. He'd already figured out what worked for him, and he did say it was only med school students, right? Grown men and women, old enough to know better, and old enough to know what they were doing.

She joined him on a landing two steps up from the dining room. They had walked to a V-shaped room, the bedroom, which was nestled into the prow of the ship. Unlike the virginal room below them, here rich, jewel-toned pillows spilled across a paisley bedspread made of raw burgundy silk, and a matching silk canopy swayed overhead. It looked like it belonged in a Bedouin's tent. "It's so beautiful," she murmured.

Eamon smiled, obviously pleased at her reaction. He pulled her close and tilted her chin. The ceiling was pure glass. "I love to fall asleep under a full moon." With that, he lowered her chin and cupped her face in his hands. He kissed her, quickly, his lips the slightest brush along hers.

She drew back in surprise. She knew where they'd been heading, she knew what he had in mind, but so many emotions overwhelmed her it was hard for her to think clearly. "Oh."

He must have sensed her reluctance, because he laughed lightly. "I've been wanting to do that since we met. C'mon, I've got more to show you."

Shaking her head to clear the fog, she followed him as he left the bedroom and made his way to the main landing, to a galley almost hidden behind the platinum-topped bar. So many emotions continued to swirl: disappointment at the news that he sold drugs during medical school, relief to be on neutral ground again, surprise that she wasn't more startled by his kiss. He grinned at her and spread his arms wide.

Compared to the rest of the yacht, especially the expansive lounge and bedroom, the kitchen looked small, with barely enough room for a compact stove, metal sink, and them, too. "It's not the Cordon Bleu, but it'll suffice."

"I'd love to help you cook." Grateful for a diversion, she poked at a cabinet door with her thumb, but it wouldn't budge.

"Here, you don't have to force it." Gently, he pressed the wood until the safety latch popped and the door swung open. "You try it."

She nodded, mimicking his movement, and this time the cabinet door opened wide. He reached around her and withdrew some pasta shells from a tall glass cylinder, which he emptied into a large skillet that sat on the stove. After igniting a flame and coaxing the water to a boil, he added a bit of olive oil, some mushrooms, and grated cheese, and began to toss the noodles like a seasoned pro.

He also began to sing—it sounded like *The Barber of Seville*—but he was a half-note away from being on pitch and he cracked on the upper octaves. That didn't stop him from blustering through three whole verses while he cooked.

"Time to eat," he finally proclaimed at the end of the third stanza.

He ushered her to one of the art deco chairs, and then returned to the galley to retrieve their meal. They ate in mannered silence, each careful to be on their best behavior. Every once in a while, she would divulge a tidbit about her family, or at least one of the good parts. The night might have continued that way—their voices never rising above a murmur—but then Eamon decided to toast the neonatologist, Dr. Cohen, who'd made a fool of himself over the hospital intercom. That led to another toast—this one for the doctor's paramour, the pediatric nurse—and that led to a series of toasts for the hospital's staff. By the time Eamon performed a near-perfect imitation of the hospital's CEO, Mr. Tennet, homespun phrases and country twang included, her sides ached from laughter.

He lowered his wine glass, leaned over his half-eaten dinner, and kissed her, long and hard. She could have lost herself in the kiss forever, but then a faint buzz sounded on the edge of her consciousness. Maybe it was a foghorn, or a timer going off in the kitchen, like the one on the oven or something else that Eamon had forgotten to turn off. But the tone grew louder—it wouldn't be ignored—the *bbbrriinngg* coming from somewhere in back of the room.

Eamon pulled away from her. "Oh, that had better not be the

ER calling."

"Actually," she had to raise her voice now to be heard, "I think it's my cell phone." The fog was beginning to lift, and the crumbled blue-jean jacket beckoned from the bar. Reluctantly, she broke away from his kiss, rose and padded over to the pile of denim lying on the bar. When she withdrew the ringing telephone, Wanda's number glowed in the tiny display window. "It's my assistant," she said, frowning. "Whatever she wants, it can't be good news."

She pushed a button on her cell phone and immediately heard Wanda's voice.

"Rhetta, where are you?" She sounded out of breath. "I've been trying to call your home for hours."

For a moment she debated telling Wanda exactly where she was, but she knew that her assistant would broadcast the news to the entire medical center in two minutes flat. "I'm eating at a friend's place tonight."

"I'll bet you're with that doctor—aren't you? I am *so sorry* . . . but I had to call you."

"Don't worry, you're not interrupting anything." Which was a lie, but why make Wanda feel any worse? "What's up?"

"It's your friend, Rhetta. The cop. The one in ICU."

It took a moment for the words to sink in.

"You still there?" Wanda asked.

"Yeah, I'm still here. What happened?"

"Well, remember how I tried to find his admitting info the other day when I was at the front desk? Only his record was blocked for some reason."

"I remember that. Why?"

"It bugged me, so I stopped by the info desk before I left work today. You know, to see if maybe I'd have better luck this time. Only when I got there and typed his name into the system, nothing came up this time. His record's gone."

"What do you mean, it's gone? How could it have disappeared?"

"Rhetta, I don't think that's the problem." Wanda's reluctance came through loud and clear. There was something else she wasn't telling her.

"Okay, Wanda . . . spill it. What do you think happened to it?"

"Go see your friend in the morning. That's all I'm saying. Look, I've got to go. Talk to you tomorrow. And I'm *really* sorry." With that, Wanda hung up, as breathless as when she first began their conversation.

Once Wanda's voice disappeared, Rhetta slowly lowered the cell phone.

"Something wrong?"

"I don't know. That was strange." She glanced over at Eamon and saw the concern in his eyes. No need to worry him, too. "Wanda told me something she found out. Guess I won't know anything until tomorrow morning."

She returned to the table and tried to muster some enthusiasm for the half-eaten dinner, but it was no use. "Look, Eamon, do you mind if I take a rain check for some other time? It's hard for me to concentrate after that."

"If that's what you want."

To her he looked more confused than irritated. She wanted to tell him everything, but at this point there wasn't much to tell. So what if Nick didn't show up as a patient in the computer record? It could have been a simple mistake. Maybe someone deleted his record by accident, or moved it to another file without thinking much about it. It could have happened to anyone, really.

"Look, why don't I take you home," Eamon said gently. "I can tell your mind's not here."

"Would you do that?" Thank God he was so understanding.

She felt as if she didn't deserve his kindness at this point, but maybe she could make it up to him.

"I know . . . let me cook for you tomorrow. It's the least I can do. We'll go to my place this time."

"Are you asking me out on a date?" he teased, a smile final broaching his lips. "Miss Day, I do declare you're being rather forward."

Not only could the man do a spot-on impersonation of Mr. Tennet, the CEO, but he did a credible Southern gentleman, as well. "I'm only asking if you're saying yes," she told him.

Tomorrow morning would come soon enough. Tomorrow morning she could visit Nick's room first thing and see for herself that nothing had changed. That Nick remained in a place full of glowing monitors and buzzing machines and virginal white bedding that scratched against her fingers when she tucked him in. All of that and more she could see once the morning light came.

Chapter 11

The red and white lights of the emergency room flickered in the dark, like a fragile beacon nestled in the shadow of the slumbering medical center. Unable to sleep more than a few hours, Rhetta finally gave up around four o'clock the next morning and navigated her way through the streets of downtown Long Beach, passing by tumbledown apartment buildings, neon liquor signs, and a pawn shop or two. The city looked dumpier than usual at this early hour, or maybe it was only her exhaustion coloring the view.

She pulled into the parking lot of the medical center, and maneuvered around an ambulance that waited under the overhang of the ER with its engine idling. The driver had nodded off behind the wheel, unaware—or unconcerned—that his ambulance was blocking the only portal to the medical center at this time of day.

She drove around it, found a parking space, and then shuffled through the sliding glass doors of the ER. A shaft of fluorescent light bounced crazily from a metal crash cart in the corner to a poster of a small girl clutching a teddy bear that hung over the triage desk.

The room smelled of ammonia and plastic wrap. A teenage boy slumped against the wall, head propped against the cream-colored surface. A makeshift sling held his left arm against his chest. Rhetta couldn't help but wonder if maybe he was a gang member. The ER director called anything after two o'clock in the morning the "witching hours," when fights that had simmered on dance floors all over town would spill over onto cracked sidewalks as soon as bartenders announced their last calls. Used to be the gang members would mix it up with switchblades and baseball bats, and then drive their fallen to the emergency room as a matter of course. But gradually the weapons got better and better, and the injuries worsened, until no one dared hang around the ER for fear they'd be hauled in by the police for questioning about a possible homicide. Nowadays, the director said, the routine usually involved a car cruising to the entrance of the ER, a door cracking open, and a body rolling out onto the pavement. So, in addition to drive-by shootings, one of the city's only emergency rooms had to contend with "roll-bys" and somehow patch up bodies that were hopelessly bloodied and bruised.

She passed the teenager on her way. Linoleum tiles, no doubt buffed by the night crew, squeaked under her heel. She paused before the nurse's desk, to talk to whichever staffer might be working now, but the desk was empty. Outside of the sullen teenager, she was the only person in the room.

Until a technician sauntered through the doorway. It was Carlos Cervantes, the former president of Nick's fraternity. His lab coat flapped open as he walked, exposing black trousers and a wrinkled t-shirt. Everything was more lax on the night shift, including the dress code, because it was one of the only ways the HR department could get people to work while the rest of the world slept, and it gave the corridors a surreal feeling after midnight. Carlos abruptly stopped when he noticed her standing there.

The sight of him startled her, too. "Carlos. I thought you worked in radiology."

"They send me all over. A little of this, a little of that." When he shook his head, a greasy lock of hair fell into his eye.

"You came for him, right?" She pointed to the dozing teenager with the injured arm.

"Yeah. He took a bullet to the elbow. Lucky they didn't aim higher." He giggled girlishly at his own joke, before turning sullen again. "What're you doing here?"

"Checking on Nick. Have you visited him yet?" It only made sense to ask, since they were fraternity buddies and all. Maybe Carlos would put aside their differences for old time's sake.

"Hell, no. Why would I do that?" He swatted at the greasy lock of hair, which had inched closer to his right eye. "If you don't remember, he's not exactly on my Christmas card list."

Of course. They had kicked Carlos out of Cal West on account of Nick. Then came the suicide attempt in the frigid ocean, and later a technician's job he obviously hated. Those were pretty strong reasons. "I thought you'd want to see him because he's so sick."

Carlos only shook his head. "I told you. For all I care that mother can take a long hike off a short pier." He caught himself at the last minute. "Not that I'd know anything about that. Besides, it looks to me like he's a goner."

"Why would you say that?" She didn't mean to sound quite so harsh, but there was no reason for Carlos to speculate like that.

"Well, I know somethin' about respiratory distress syndrome. A lot of people don't pull through it. Hell, his chart's a mess."

"How'd you see his electronic chart?"

Carlos grinned. "Someone sure blew it when they gave Nick that thyroid test. How could *that* have happened? You have to be so careful these days. They'll let just about anybody work on the patients . . . anybody at all."

"I said . . . how did you see his record?" Even though there was no possible way Nick's doctor would have given Carlos access to the computer record, someone else must have.

"You're not his doctor, why do you care? Besides, I've got work to do. That guy's arm ain't gonna X-ray itself."

Carlos turned his back on her and swaggered over to the groggy teenager. Rhetta felt like grabbing him by the shoulder and shaking him, but that would only cause a scene. Plus, she distinctly remembered Susannah Vandermeer urging her to ignore Carlos. She'd called him "mental," or something like that.

So Rhetta lowered her head and left the emergency room. She studied the carpet all the way across the darkened lobby to the bank of elevators. Hopefully the charge nurse upstairs would let her in to see Nick, even though visiting hours technically wouldn't start until eight o'clock. Maybe she could claim to be working on a story, or scouting locations for a news reporter, or checking in on Nick for his wife. Anything to make the woman—or man—say yes.

When she arrived at the elevator, she was surprised to see someone else standing there. A man of about fifty, with a slim tape recorder in his hand, had beaten her to the spot. She knew at a glance the type of equipment a radio reporter used, and that machine fit the bill.

"Can I help you?"

"Sure," he said. In reality, the man did *not* look sure, given the way he eyed her up and down. "I'm on my way to the PR department. Do you know what time they get in?"

"Usually there's no one there until eight. Are you on a deadline?"

"Yeah, I need to file for the morning drive time."

"I can probably help. Just tell me what it's about." As if she didn't know. Odds were good the reporter wanted to follow up on the story about Dr. Visser after yesterday's disastrous press conference.

"The operation on the city councilman. I'm looking for an update."

"Well, I'm Rhetta Day from the PR department. It's not upstairs . . . we can go across the hall to my office. Follow me."

She led him down the executive corridor to where the PR department lay. What she wanted to do was make her way up to the intensive care unit to visit Nick, and not to babysit a radio reporter at this ungodly hour.

She flicked on the lights once they stood inside her office. Wordlessly, she pointed to a chair pushed up against the darkened window. She couldn't help but feel sorry for the stranger, because while it took a crisis to get her up so early, for him this was probably routine.

"Test, test, test." The man practically touched the machine to his lips. "This is Austin Rivers, live in Long Beach, for KMX."

When she first began in PR, she found it strange that reporters tested their equipment with a sign-off, until someone finally spelled it out for her. The person explained that reporters do so to save on time. If nothing else, a reporter would have his sign-off recorded before even getting started, and then he could edit it to the end of the report later.

The man cleared his throat, and slid the tape recorder onto her desk. "We understand there's no change in Councilman Griago's condition. Can you tell our listeners what happened?"

She almost said no comment, but that tired phrase had been used far too often for her to feel good about it. "The hospital is conducting an investigation to determine why the councilman's surgery turned out the way it did. We'll have more to say once the investigation's complete."

After spending a few years working in public relations and countless hours trapped in an auditorium at Cal West listening to lectures on public relations and crisis communications before that, the words rolled right off her tongue.

"How is the family taking this?"

A surgeon botched the guy's operation . . . how do you think they're taking it? That's what she wanted to ask him.

"I can't comment on that because I haven't personally spoken to the family. Any answer from me at this point would be speculation."

That's it; keep asking inane questions, she wanted to urge him. The further they roamed from the subject of Dr. Visser, the better. *Dr. Visser.* She hadn't thought of him since the night before. He'd probably risen by now and was prepping for his first surgery of the day.

The reporter reached over to flick off the tape recorder.

"Wait a minute," she said, stopping him. "I want to make another statement." She drew the machine closer. "The hospital deeply regrets this turn of events. We're doing everything we can to find out what happened, and why."

The moment she finished speaking, she worried about her choice of words. If the reporter wanted to, he could twist them around to sound like an admission of guilt; especially if he implied that in the story's lead-in. Oh well . . . she could blame her chattiness on the early hour or on her lack of sleep. Next time she'd tell Arianna to go lie for herself, because it was only five o'clock in the morning and already she wanted to dive right back into bed.

"Here's my card," the man said. "I may want a follow-up."

She accepted the paper warily. Her shoulders ached, and through the picture window, across the parking lot, the chunky silhouette of the medical center mocked her. The lights remained off in most of the rooms, except for a row of gleaming rectangles that highlighted the top floor. The nurses there didn't bother to turn off the lights as they filed in and out, busy with their trays and their needles and their bottles of codeine. No need, since their patients weren't awake to notice anyway. Up there was Nick and his tennis shoes. Attached to a machine that breathed for him and a tube that jutted from his mouth like a bizarre appendage.

She barely noticed when the reporter slipped away. After a moment, she also rose and began to walk out of the public relations office, finally free to ride the elevator to the seventh floor and check on Nick.

Once in the lobby she could tell the hospital was starting to come alive. Clusters of people milled around, chatting. Everyone looked so fresh and alert at this early hour, starched and combed, their faces full of hope. But she knew that by the end of the day the strain of dealing with sickness and grief would recast them. Tension would wear away at the visitors' eagerness and dull their smiles, as inevitably as the air conditioner would evaporate their freshly applied perfumes and colognes.

She waited for the main elevator, and when it arrived, slouched to the back of the car, behind a hospital orderly. When the door closed, she felt a twinge of guilt. She belonged back in her office, doing the job they paid her to do, but it was impossible to concentrate without knowing Nick's status. Without knowing what had upset Wanda so the night before. She finally exhaled when the elevator heaved past the third floor, then the sixth, and exposed the lobby of the ICU.

Compared to the lobby downstairs, the waiting area for the intensive care unit was empty. No eager smiles, no hopeful looks, no brightly colored balloons here. Only two rows of functional vinyl chairs, separated by a molded plastic end table or two. Even the potted ferns looked plastic. She approached the receptionist's desk, but before she reached it, a man hurtling out of the swinging doors nearly knocked her down.

"Oh! I'm sorry."

The stranger wore a white lab coat and a hospital badge. "No problem," she told him, noticing a clutch of file folders in his hand.

"Didn't mean to run right into you."

"Really . . . it's okay." Given the absence of a stethoscope, the man couldn't be a doctor. Maybe someone from laboratory, or radiology, or the pharmacy department.

"I've got to get this stuff back to pharmacy," he said.

Bingo. "So you've been on the unit? Were you all alone?" With a little luck, maybe she'd have some peace and privacy to visit with Nick.

"I don't know, because I had to turn around. Don't know what it's like in there today."

Something about his quiet demeanor impressed Rhetta. Didn't an OR charge nurse once tell her that pharmacists held all of the power at the hospital? That they were the ones—not the doctors, or the surgeons, or the charge nurses, even—who knew the ins and outs of the medical center? It was worth a shot.

"Say, do you know the patients on the unit? By the way, I'm Rhetta Day, from the PR department. I have a friend in there. His name is Nick Tahari. Know him?"

"Tahari? Sure. He's one of the youngest patients on the unit right now." He blanched, as if it hurt him personally to see someone like Nick in the intensive care unit. "Most of our patients are cardiac cases, and they're usually a lot older. Wasn't he a policeman?"

"He is—" she started to correct him, but gave up. "Yeah. He was with the police department." How Nick had struggled before the physical, nibbling carrot sticks and jogging down the beach path before sunrise. He'd even given up Friday nights at The Corner Pocket for a while. He did it, though; when it came time to take the police department physical, he breezed through it as if it was only a morning run on the beach.

"I'm sorry." The pharmacist flipped open his notepad and riffled through a few pages.

Even upside down, Rhetta could tell the writing was shorthand. Wavy lines took the place of whole words and extra white space separated the squiggles. After a moment, he looked up again.

"The diagnosis was full-blown respiratory distress brought on by a severe allergic reaction." The man studied the words again before speaking. "He took the radioactive tracer for a thyroid scan. You have to be so careful with iodine."

"Do you keep notes on all your patients?"

"I prefer a hard copy. The electronic records are great, but I remember things better if I write them on paper. No one sees this but me."

"What else does it say?"

"Well, it looks like they did everything right," he told her. "They started him on epinephrine, gave him IV with saline. He even came around for a while, before respiratory distress set in."

Rhetta could hear the elevator doors whoosh open behind her, so she knew that someone had joined them in the lobby. This might be the only time she had the pharmacist's undivided attention, and she didn't want to waste it.

"Go on . . . do you know what happened?"

"There was some cardiac distress, too. He got almost two hundred fifty microcuries of iodine. That's a lot higher than we usually use." He glanced away from the notes, briefly. "There's not as much oversight at some of those smaller hospitals. We usually top out at fifty microcuries."

"You're right, Andrew." Eamon's voice boomed from somewhere close behind them.

They both turned to see the doctor, who wore maroon scrubs

yet again, and a bright smile. "I appreciate your diligence on this case."

"But . . . it's no problem." Eamon's entrance had caused the pharmacist to shrink back into his lab coat, as if the cloth would protect him from the larger man. "I find it fascinating."

"I'm sure you do. Hi there, Rhetta." Gently, he bent down and kissed her cheek.

"We were talking about Nick's diagnosis. Is anything new?"

"I don't know yet. Just got here," Eamon said. "Had to prep for a case this morning. Thought I'd drop in on him, too, to see how he was coming along. Yesterday there was a rumor he might go to a specialty hospital if things don't look better." He turned sideways, which effectively blocked the pharmacist from their conversation. "I know they're keeping him on oxygen and meds."

The pharmacist cleared his throat, but Eamon didn't budge.

"The sedation will give his lungs a chance to heal."

Apparently, the pharmacist had something to say, because he peered at her over Eamon's shoulder. "There are a few other tests they could consider."

"We've covered them all." Finally, Eamon turned and addressed the soft-spoken man. He spoke with exaggerated patience, as a father would lecture a precocious son. "I think his physicians know what they're doing, Mr. Wong, so you don't have to worry about this case."

"Whatever you say, Doctor." Although the man seemed to want to say more, he shrank away from Eamon. Any confidence he might have felt before the doctor joined them had slowly ebbed away. "Well, it was nice to meet you, Miss Day. Maybe we'll run into each other again."

"Sure. You never know who you'll bump into around here."

She sounded too chipper, and she knew it. As soon as the pharmacist walked away, she turned on Eamon.

"You made him nervous, you know." She should have been

used to the differential tone people used around doctors, but still it bothered her.

"I didn't mean to. I'll bet everyone makes him nervous. How are things downstairs?"

"I wouldn't know. I left about half an hour ago." Who knew how many messages were waiting for her by now? Arianna had probably ordered Wanda to track her down, like a hound dog on a scent, and it wouldn't be the first time. "I must be losing my touch. Putting a happy face on things used to be a whole lot easier."

"Well, the phone calls aren't going to go away, so you might as well face the music. I'll let you know what goes on up here." He slid his arm around her shoulders. "Try not to worry about Nick. Oh . . . and I think you owe me dinner tonight."

"You're right. I do. Maybe I'll pop in and say hello to Nick and then head back downstairs."

"You're too early for visiting hours, Rhetta. Trust me. I'll let you know if anything changes. Now, about that dinner. I'm a fool for pasta. You know that."

"Pasta? Oh yeah, I remember. Why don't you show up at my house around eight? It's not as fancy as your boat, but it'll do."

"Sounds good. I'm looking forward to it. You head back to work and I'll check on Nick. And use plenty of olive oil. I like my pasta nice and slick."

She couldn't help but smile back at him. He seemed so energetic, so full of life, and damned if he didn't have the most beautiful aqua eyes she'd ever seen. Such a lucky girl to call this handsome stranger a friend.

He kissed her once more—this time on the lips—and reluctantly she retreated from the relative quiet of the waiting room.

CHAPTER 12

After saying good-bye to Eamon, Rhetta returned to the PR office, where she hoped to find Wanda. She always could count on her assistant to fill her in with the latest news, especially if it involved Arianna.

But Wanda's chair was empty and pushed flush with the desk. Manila file folders and telephone messages, all unfiled, splayed across the surface. No doubt Wanda was on another "errand" . . . maybe for the rest of the morning.

Rhetta rummaged around on the desk for messages. She found six of hers, and scanned them as she retreated to her office. She took a few steps, before a voice interrupted her reading.

"Where have you been?" Normally Arianna wore a well-practiced smile, even when delivering the worst of news, but not now. She stood with her back to Rhetta's window, her silhouette blotting the light. "You were supposed to be here early. Answering calls. That *is* your job, isn't it?"

"Of course. It's just that I—"

"Whatever." Arianna flicked her hand. "They've called a special meeting of the board of directors in five minutes. We need to move fast, before this thing with Dr. Visser explodes. I trust you can make it?"

It wasn't a question, and Rhetta knew that, so she nodded.

"Good, I thought so. For some reason, the board wants your

input. So try not to go anywhere. I hope I can count on you this time."

"No problem." Should she say anything to Arianna about the radio reporter she met up with in the lobby? About how she might have said too much? Or would it be better to let the chips fall where they may? Either way, she felt much too tired to care. "Look, I have to return these phone calls."

"All right, then. See you in five minutes."

With that, Arianna stomped away. Rhetta felt like tossing the papers in her hand into the trash, but instead, she dropped them on the desk and reached for the telephone receiver. After dialing, a sugary voice came on the line.

"Pharmacy."

"Hi, this is Rhetta Day, from PR. I'm looking for a pharmacist by the name of Wong."

"Haven't seen him." Before she could protest, the voice spoke again. "I'll check, though."

Rhetta riffled through the messages while she waited. It seemed that everyone had called her, from reporters working at L.A.'s dailies to people she'd never heard of. There was even one from a newspaper in Redlands. Redlands? Who knew they had a daily, let alone would bother to call on a story they'd picked up from the wire service. Of course, everyone subscribed to the wire, and it was easier to follow up on an existing story than to poke around for new leads. Next thing she knew, she'd get a call from the *California Enquirer,* of all things. What was taking the pharmacist so long?

"Andrew Wong."

"Hey Mr. Wong, this is Rhetta Day. We met a few minutes ago in ICU?"

"Oh, right. Mr. Tahari's friend."

"Yeah." Rhetta walked around her desk, and gingerly lifted the extension cord over its paper-strewn surface. "Look, I wanted to ask you a couple of questions earlier. Are you free now?"

"I guess so."

"Great." She paused. Something was bothering her, and had been since she left the ICU. "It's about my friend. You said he had an allergic reaction to a test. What kind of a test?" Nervously she twisted the telephone cord around her index finger. Patients' records were confidential—she knew that—and he had every right to tell her it was none of her business.

"Hmmm . . . wasn't it a thyroid scan? Yeah, I'm pretty sure."

"Is that common? Common for someone like Nick, I mean?" She continued to wrap the cord around her finger, certain he would cut her off.

"It's not a common test for someone his age, but it does happen. The symptoms are usually fatigue or lethargy."

"Oh. You said there was a reaction. An allergy."

"That's right." The pharmacist's voice rose; her questions seemed to give him confidence. Perhaps no one ever asked for his opinion. "The radioisotope they use is iodine. We usually get about two hundred and fifty microcopies a day from food, but give that same amount to someone who's allergic and you never know how they'll react." He sounded energized now. "Unfortunately, people sometimes don't know how the isotope will affect them until it's too late. You could have everything from mild nausea to cardiac distress. There's really no telling."

"I see." Rhetta paused, hoping he'd continue. He was on a roll and she didn't dare interrupt him.

"Here at St. James we're extremely careful. We use only the lowest dose possible. Usually not more than fifty microcuries. A hundred, tops. Course, we pay more for it, too. It costs us more for those lower-level isotopes, but we think it's worth it."

"I agree. I don't suppose I could see Nick's electronic chart some time?" Her voice trailed; she knew full well the pharmacist would say no.

"That's impossible." He sounded apologetic. "Hospital policy. You know, we have to follow the rules."

"It's okay. You've been a big help already. Thank you."

"Any time." The man paused, and for an instant, Rhetta thought he might change his mind. "Well, good-bye then."

She hung up the handset, lost in thought, but a moment later the machine jangled. The sound broke her reverie and yanked her away from the intensive care unit and back down to her own office.

She hesitated before lifting the receiver.

"Rhetta?" It was Larry Belknap, of all people. She hadn't spoken to him since reading the article in the *Los Angeles Examiner.* "How ya doin'?"

Funny, but he didn't sound like a man under investigation. In fact, he sounded positively upbeat. "I'm okay, I guess. How are you?"

"Been better. Been better. Got myself in a little hot water over here. Nothin' I can't handle."

From the little she'd heard about Larry, she'd have to agree with him. Nick had once said that Larry could worm his way out of anything, given enough time. He called the man a magician. "Yeah, I saw the article. You still on the force? They didn't suspend you, did they?"

"Nah, nothin' like that. They're goin' on thin air. I know it'll blow over." He inhaled deeply, as if steeling himself for whatever came next. "You talk to Nick yet?"

"What? Oh, no. I saw him yesterday, but he was asleep. Why?"

"Curious, is all. Can't a partner worry about his buddy?" He laughed lightly.

"He's about the same, maybe a little worse. They're talking about transferring him now."

"Really? Well, if that's what it takes."

"It's only talk at this point."

"According to my wife, Nick's in for one helluva fight."

She didn't know Larry well enough to picture a wife or children, or anything outside of the police force. "Your wife?"

"Yeah. She works at the local community hospital, down in radiology. She sees some tough cases, boy."

Rhetta paused. Something clicked into place, like the final piece of a jigsaw puzzle. "That's where they gave Nick the medicine for his test. Does she know him?"

"Nah, I don't think she does. But will you call me if anything changes with Nick? Anything at all. I usually work nights, so don't worry about calling too late."

"Just a second," she said. Like a jigsaw piece that had finally found its way home. "Are you sure your wife doesn't know Nick? He was there the other night—"

"Look, I've gotta get going. They've been watching me like a hawk ever since that timesheet baloney. Stay in touch, okay?"

He hung up so quickly that Rhetta didn't have time to ask another question. Maybe Larry's wife was there the night Nick took the medicine for his test. Maybe she knew what had happened to send his body into respiratory distress. Maybe she finally could tell Rhetta how something like that was even possible. Wouldn't that be something?

She returned the telephone receiver to its cradle. Interesting that Larry would call her so early, especially since he worked the night shift. Whatever could he be thinking?

She pondered that as she rose from the desk and left her office. She'd have to jog to the boardroom if she wanted to make it on time, and as she sped along the executive corridor, the wallpaper passed in a blur.

The elegant corridor finally deposited her in an equally grand space. Rich mahogany panels encased the walls of the boardroom, and an onyx table that had to be at least eight feet long ran the length of it.

She wasn't surprised to find herself alone. At her first meeting there, in the "inner sanctum," she'd marveled when the hospital's board members arrived ten, twenty, or even thirty minutes late. Then, as if on cue, the no-shows would bunch through the doorway in a group, with overstuffed briefcases crammed under their arms. They didn't even bother to apologize for being late to the meeting. It dawned on her then that the richer and more powerful the board member, the later they came. As if they couldn't possibly be bothered with something as insignificant as time . . . especially if it was other people's time. She shrugged, and flopped into the nearest chair.

Surprisingly enough, after a few minutes, Arianna walked in, only a fraction late. She appraised the space, strode to the head of the table, and sat down. "Whatcha doing way down there?"

"I've been up since four."

"That right? Well, you don't have to hide way down there. These men don't bite. You may even learn something from them. I found out a long time ago you can't let these people intimidate you. Maybe we should rehearse what we're going to say."

What was there to say? They were all there for the same reason and they knew it—damage control. "What would you like me to say?" She hoped the sarcasm would come across, but that was doubtful.

"Well, I suggest we follow Mr. Tennet's lead. Our CEO will probably want a press release first thing, maybe a briefing for the board. Lord help us if he wants another live press conference. Unfortunately, the camera doesn't seem to favor our chief executive."

At that moment, Mr. Tennet walked through the door. He wore a knotted lanyard around his neck made of faded cowhide, and his white hair fluttered untamed around his face. He was such a sight for Rhetta's weary eyes. Here he was, head of a multibillion-dollar hospital, and he didn't bother to dress up for a board of directors meeting. The lanyard even hung crooked around his neck.

She smiled at him. He might have been a character, but he was true to himself. She knew exactly where she stood with him, which was a lot more than she could say about most people at the medical center.

He returned the smile, and only then did she glance down at an agenda someone had placed on the table. The usual headings had been typed in the usual order: *Introductions. Discussion. Action Items.* Three-quarters of the way down the page, under a section called *Solutions,* someone had typed her name, in all capital letters, no less, right next to the name of the chairman of the board.

Why, Arianna hadn't said one word to her about speaking at this meeting. Not one word. Let alone about her preceding the most powerful person there. She shouldn't have been surprised, though, because it was just like Arianna to sign her up for something she had no intention of doing herself.

Rhetta didn't have time to protest, though, because a stream of people had begun to file into the boardroom. She recognized many of them from the hospital's monthly newsletter. There were a few bankers, a couple of lawyers, and one doctor. She'd heard they only elected him to the board to placate the medical staff and rarely took his opinions seriously.

When the door opened again, the chairman of the board rushed in and took his position behind the podium. To be honest, she'd never quite trusted Mr. Harrington. With his piercing eyes and his Roman nose, he reminded her of a nighthawk poised to swoop down on its unsuspecting prey.

"We're getting questions, gentlemen. Lots of questions." He

glanced at Arianna and then at her, but didn't bother to correct himself. Turns out he'd launched right into the discussion portion of the agenda without even bothering to make introductions. "It doesn't look good, not at all. What if we say we had a breakdown in communications here? That's a good line, and we can use it. Something could have happened in the OR before Dr. Visser even got there."

Amazing. He had already decided the best course of action was to sacrifice another employee in Dr. Visser's place. Who would it be? The X-ray tech? A surgical nurse? Or, maybe a radiology resident in her first year who'd be naive enough to think the hospital would never rewrite history to save a doctor. That person, whoever he or she was, didn't stand a chance against the men in this room.

Mr. Harrington motioned to the doorway then, to a figure that had moved there. "I brought in a witness today. I think he has something very interesting to say."

At that, Eamon McAllister—of all people—sauntered into the room. He wore the same bright smile she'd seen up in the ICU, as if he were perfectly at ease here. Whatever was he doing in the boardroom?

"Gentlemen." His gaze flitted over to her. "And ladies. I'm Eamon McAllister."

Around her, the high-backed chairs squeaked as board members shifted impatiently. This audience wasn't used to waiting for anything, and they didn't suffer long-windedness. He'd have to speak quickly if he wanted to hold their attention. She realized then that she was rooting for him. When had that started? When did she begin to care how Eamon appeared to others? Something about him—about them—had changed.

"What happened to this patient was tragic," he began.

Good for him. Those were nice, strong words. Something the audience could appreciate.

"You see, there's nothing to worry about," he continued. "The way I look at it, it was a tragic mistake. The films were obviously turned the wrong way, or the tech switched the X-ray markers. Mistakes do happen."

He must have heard something from one of the nurses, or from the tech who was in surgery that morning. *That must be it.* He must have learned, on his own, that nothing unusual had taken place during the councilman's operation.

"You see, I assisted that morning. I was there." He spread his arms wide. "There's no way Dr. Visser was impaired, because he looked fine to me."

The shuffling, the creaking chairs, the watchful eyes of Mr. Harrington . . . it all fell away. What did he mean, he assisted that day? That was impossible. He would have said something to her by now, only he hadn't. So it mustn't be true.

"Don't you mean you *know* who assisted?" She spoke just loud enough for the people around her to hear. "You know who assisted that morning, right? C'mon Eamon, tell them."

Slowly, Eamon shook his head. "No, Rhetta, I was there. Dr. Visser is a fine surgeon. He never would have gone into the operating room impaired. Never."

She remembered the two of them on his sailboat, where they'd huddled over a glassy cocktail table and had shared their secrets for well over an hour. He'd had ample time to tell her about the surgery. "We're talking about the councilman, Eamon. You must be thinking about someone else."

"No, Rhetta. I assisted Dr. Visser. Didn't I tell you?"

No, you didn't tell me, she wanted to scream. But before she could make sense of his words, before anything else, something stirred at her shoulder. Mr. Tennet's assistant had walked up behind her chair, and had curtly dropped a note on the table in front of her.

It was a telephone message. Something about the ICU, followed by a four-digit number. Gradually, the words came into focus, the faces and noises around her solidified, and she realized the message was about Nick.

What were they talking about? She felt as if she'd been dredged from a deep sleep. Who were these men, and why were they staring at her? What did they expect her to say?

The board's only physician leaned toward her. "Come on. They're waiting for you."

Clumsily, she rose to her feet. She could hear an intercom somewhere in the hall, but it sounded like the speaker's mouth was stuffed with cotton. She could see Eamon, staring at her from the head of the table. Arianna, who looked annoyed with her yet again. Who were these people, and what did they expect from her? "I'm sorry. I got some news. What were you saying?"

Mr. Harrington rolled his eyes. When he spoke, he stressed each word. "I asked if you had plans for the media, Miss Day."

"Right now we're responding to their calls." Her cheeks grew warm, and her words leapfrogged one ahead of the other. "We're telling them 'no comment.' There's not—"

" 'No comment' looks like an admission of guilt." Just like a nighthawk, the chairman of the board had apparently zeroed in on his prey . . . and it was her.

"I'm sorry. I can't do this." She couldn't breathe, and she needed to reach the bright hall outside. That much was real. That much she knew.

She fled the room in two long strides, leaving behind a dozen gawking men and Arianna, who also looked stunned. She had to flee the questioning looks, the stale air, the feeling of being buried alive.

Rushing through the corridor, she aimed for the stairwell. Once there, she took the steps two at a time. A wall of mirrors separated each floor, and she saw her reflection between the second and third floors. Her face looked crazed, her eyes wild with fear, but it didn't matter. She resumed her climb, and when she arrived at the seventh floor, panting, she flung open the metal door.

The receptionist's desk sat empty. She saw a bright orange telephone on the counter and lunged for it. After two muddled attempts, with fingers trembling and heart pounding, she managed to dial Nick's room, but the line was busy.

So she slammed the receiver down and hurried into the hall, ignoring a sign that read "staff only." Someone yelled at her to stop, but the voice echoed as if relayed through a tin can. She couldn't respond; she couldn't do anything but punch a button in the wall to activate the door to the ICU.

Which she bolted through, and then stopped in front of Nick's room. Something was wrong. Terribly wrong. The room felt far too quiet. She knew inside, before it fully registered in her mind, that something was missing.

The irritating beep of the cardiac monitor had vanished. Same with the wheeze of the respirator. Compared to the nervous activity that rippled from the room next door, Nick's room seemed cavernous, hollow.

She peered inside. Everything *looked* the same. The faded chair still crouched in the corner, flanked by an IV pole and yards of PVC tube. The place smelled of rubbing alcohol, nothing new there. But the bed. The side rails were down, and the pristine sheets lay flat where Nick's sleeping form should have been. She edged closer, but there was no denying that the bed lay empty.

"Rhetta." A voice floated over to her. It was Andrew Wong, the pharmacist. "I'm so sorry. I only now found out."

She stared at him. "Where's Nick?" Had he been transferred? Was he in a different room? Maybe he'd been sent to another floor.

"He's gone. It must have happened late last night."

"Gone? Is he having more tests?"

"No Rhetta, he's not having more tests."

Everything slowed. A thousand images crowded into her mind and then quickly disappeared. She could picture Nick's black tennis shoes. High-tops, they were. He had to be ready for a quick game of one-on-one basketball, don't you know. She could see his scratchy writing on a sticky note. *Scared as hell.* The way he'd turned the pad upside down to make it easier for her to read. Why was the pharmacist staring at her like that?

"Are you okay?" he asked.

"Yeah, I think so." It didn't sound like her voice at all. She had to keep talking, though, because every time she formed a word, the pounding in her ears softened. "What now?"

"Nothing. There's nothing anyone could do. He wasn't strong enough."

"I know." Somehow, she did know. It didn't make sense; he had every chance to get better. But when she first saw Nick's waxy face, cradled by the starched white pillow, she knew. When she saw sweat beads against his upper lip, saw the waxy sheen on his cheeks and chin, she knew. The pharmacist moved to her side and touched her shoulder, tentatively. He expected her to say something. But what? She didn't feel anything yet.

"Are you going to be all right?"

"I'd like a minute. Alone." For some absurd reason, she felt the need to reassure the soft-spoken man standing next to her. "I'll be fine." She tried to smile, but could only manage a tight-lipped grimace.

"All right, then. I'll leave you alone."

Only when the pharmacist's steps grew faint did she lower her head. She began to sob—quietly at first—and then with such fervor that she worried she might never stop.

CHAPTER 13

Rhetta spent the rest of the day only half aware of the sights and sounds around her. Eventually, she returned to her office, where random papers and telephone messages littered the desk. At some point she'd have to deal with the real world—she knew that—but not now.

"Rhetta?"

She turned to see Eamon standing under the threshold of her doorway.

"I just heard about Nick. I'm *so* sorry." He looked sorry, with his shoulders hunched forward like that.

"Oh, Eamon." What could she say? Her worst fear had come true. She'd dreaded this moment from the very first day, and the pain was overwhelming.

"Come over here." He opened his arms wide, and beckoned her to join him.

She hesitated, but then threw herself into his arms. His shoulders felt so strong when he wrapped himself around her like that. They blocked out everything . . . the sunlight, the sound of voices, the smell of copy paper and ink. They enveloped her so completely she almost didn't hear the sobs that came from her own throat.

The last time she'd sobbed like this, she'd been a little girl in her grandmother's lap. She'd listened while her favorite person in the whole-wide-world told her something ugly and hurtful. Something that couldn't possibly be true. How could her parents have died in a fiery car crash? What did her grandmother mean when she said they'd loved her, but now they couldn't be with her? That didn't make any sense. If her parents really loved her, they would come back to her and her gramma, and then she wouldn't have to hear such horrible things.

"You'll be fine," she heard Eamon say now. Gently, he stroked her hair, which made her want to cry all the harder. "But you need to get away from here for a while. Come on with me."

He didn't wait for her answer, but took her by the hand and led her out of the office. Past Wanda's desk—which sat empty, thankfully—and then past the oil paintings in the executive hall and the hustle and bustle of the lobby, which never seemed to close. She didn't say one word during their entire journey, until they stood in the parking lot and she realized she'd forgotten her purse and had absolutely nothing on her but the clothes on her back and a cell phone in her pocket.

"Wait. Eamon, I forgot my purse—"

"You won't need it," he told her, as he opened the door to his convertible and eased her into it. "We can get your things tomorrow."

Silently, they pulled away. At the first stoplight, her breath finally even now, she remembered why she'd hesitated, back there in her office, when Eamon had first appeared. The board meeting. The chairman of the board. Introducing someone who could help them understand what'd happened with Dr. Visser. Because Eamon was there the morning of the city councilman's surgery.

When the light didn't change, she spoke up. "Eamon, why didn't you tell me you assisted with Dr. Visser's surgery that morning?"

"I don't know. Would it have changed anything?"

"You should have told me."

"I didn't want you to think I was covering for him. That

wasn't it at all. The doctor looked fine. I swear, if he was doing drugs, I couldn't tell."

She wanted to believe him. Watching him now, he seemed so confident. So very sure of himself.

They lapsed back into silence once the light changed, while the air swirled around them and filled the spaces in between. After a while, they arrived at the same pier she'd seen the night before, the one with masts that jutted high into the sky and had improbably tied rigging that looked like ropes for a circus tent.

Once again, she smelled saltwater and fishing tackle, motor oil and teakwood polish, and it comforted her. After driving into a parking space, Eamon climbed out of the sports car and helped her to do the same. When they arrived at the dock, he scooped her into his arms and deposited her on the deck of his boat, which lolled about like a baby's cradle.

She would be safe here, if only for a while. He carried her aboard, through the dining room, past the mahogany cocktail tables, and then under the length of sparkling ceiling. Finally, he gently laid her on the couch and nodded toward the bar.

"Can I fix you something?" It was the first time he'd spoken since she'd asked him about the surgery. For some reason, she didn't hesitate. It was probably only three o'clock in the afternoon—bright afternoon sun glowed behind the window shades—but she didn't care.

She nodded yes and he began to fix them both martinis. He returned to her side with the drinks and offered one to her, which she gladly accepted.

Neither felt compelled to talk as they sipped their drinks and watched the sun inch across the hardwood floors. The cool liquid bathed her throat and untwined the knot lodged between her shoulders. When they'd finished, he placed her glass on the floor, scooped her up off the couch, and wordlessly carried her into his bedroom. Tenderly, he laid her on the lavender bedspread: the magic carpet of his Bedouin's tent.

She was so tired. So very, very tired. Even with the beautiful surroundings, the velvet pillows and sparkling glass ceiling, and his gorgeous eyes trained on her face, her own eyes felt leaden. "I'm exhausted, Eamon."

"Shhh. Get some rest. I understand."

He settled in beside her, and draped his arm across her back. Within a few minutes she fell fast asleep and felt herself floating away from the boat. Floating toward the hospital, where every light still burned in the intensive care unit and every machine still glowed in Nick's room. She dreamt that nothing had changed at all. There were still tests to be run at the special clinic, still scans to be read, there was still time. Time to change everything.

Much, much later, the ringing of a telephone awoke her. The bedroom was dark, and she felt Eamon's arm along her back. She twisted and reluctantly edged out from under the warm covers, followed the sound to the bar, where she'd dropped her cell phone on the counter, and flipped the machine open groggily, only half-awake.

"Rhetta Day?" The speaker had a husky, smoky voice.

"Yes. Can I help you?" *Please, not a reporter. Not now.*

"Nick's wife asked me to call." The name jarred her awake. When she didn't respond, the stranger cleared his throat, but the hoarseness remained. "I worked with him. I'm calling about his funeral."

She looked around the darkened cabin. How long had she been asleep? Amazingly, time had passed while she lay in Eamon's bed. The world could have collapsed outside and she wouldn't have known, or to be honest, have cared.

"His funeral will be Monday at St. Stephen's. At oh-eight-hundred hours. I'm sure he wanted you to be there."

She realized then that the caller was a policeman. Only a

lieutenant or a sergeant would spell out the time for her in military hours. He probably thought she was an idiot, though, because she hadn't said anything yet. "Monday?" she finally whispered.

"Yes, in four days."

She remembered, too late, to thank the stranger before he hung up. *In four days.* Funerals happened quickly, everyone knew that, but this seemed so sudden. The man had said something about St. Stephen's. Wasn't that the church with the marble arches, grimacing gargoyles, and medieval-looking turrets, so dark and foreboding? So formal, so very imposing and *so* unlike Nick.

She sank to the carpet and wrapped her arms around her chest, suddenly cold. The only time she and Nick had ever talked about funerals was back in college, one night before the end of their final semester together. What had brought about that conversation was anyone's guess, but Nick had asked her, point blank, how she wanted to "go" when her time came. She'd tried to be funny—where was she supposed to go?—but he looked completely serious, so she decided to play along, and made up a story about scattering her ashes on the beach at sunset, because it was the only thing she could think of and she'd never been asked *that* question before. It was something she'd never thought about. She'd never been to a funeral, not even that of her parents, because her grandmother feared it would give her nightmares.

She remembered how Nick had chuckled when she told him her plans. It was perfect for her, but not for him, he'd said. No, he wanted a boozy wake—think of New Orleans—with trumpet riffs and cigarette smoke and a conga line. That's what he wanted, or so he said.

He had it all worked out. He told her, with a straight face, that people used to drink wine from lead cups hundreds of years ago. After a few too many glasses, a chemical reaction between the alcohol and lead would knock them out cold. Their families couldn't exactly bury them, because who knew if they were really dead? So they'd hold a boozy wake to make sure the dear departed didn't return. He loved that story. Yep; lay me out and make sure I'm a goner, he'd said. Have a party while you're at it so the noise will bring me back.

Awkwardly, she rose from the floor. He wouldn't be getting his wish. Didn't Beryl know that Nick hated big, formal churches and how he had to dress for them? He loathed solemn, officious occasions, and solemn, officious places. Beryl should have known that. In the end, Nick wouldn't even get the funeral he'd hoped for.

Ever the gentleman, Eamon drove her to her office, where she retrieved her purse, and then he insisted on following behind as she drove home to her apartment. He even waited patiently at the curb while she fumbled with her keys and unlocked the front door. Thankfully, he'd agreed to postpone their dinner date until a few nights later.

To be honest, the apartment seemed unusually cold and uninviting, but somewhere along the line she'd lost the will to be polite. She couldn't imagine spending one more second worried about what Eamon would think or what he would say if she lost it again and burst into tears. So she faked a smile for his benefit and waved, and then watched the taillights of his car disappear.

Maybe it was time for dinner. Heaven only knew that she hadn't eaten in forever. But the thought of cooking something—anything—exhausted her. Even warming a box of macaroni and cheese would take too much thought and too much effort.

Left with few options, she decided to back out the door the way she'd come and softly shut it behind her. She knew what

Nick would do. When in doubt, he'd go for bright lights, lots of noise, and a beer or two. That seemed to be his panacea for most everything, and tonight it made sense. She needed a place to blur the picture in her mind of Nick's empty hospital bed, and the way the pharmacist tried to comfort her, to no avail. To forget about Beryl's misguided plans for his funeral. Somewhere she could remain anonymous and no one would care if her eyes suddenly misted, her voice cracked, or a tear slid down her cheek. She wanted to leave herself behind, if only for a while.

So she yanked the car keys from her pocket. She'd go to the last place she'd seen Nick in all of his blustery glory. Someplace where no one ever got sick and nothing bad ever happened. The Corner Pocket. The bar where she and Nick had spent hours talking about everything and nothing at all. A place so distracting she couldn't help but lose herself.

Once she drove away from the apartment, it took her only five minutes to reach the bar, where a neon sign above its entrance blinked on and off sporadically, and an electrified martini glass sputtered in a corner.

Nothing had changed, of course. A row of shiny motorcycles still leaned into each other in the first few parking spaces and the bar's weathered gray planks needed a paint job.

And despite the glow from the flickering neon sign, black film still covered the windows to prevent any tourists or teenagers from peering inside. To get into the bar, patrons were forced to take a sharp turn at the door, then zigzag to the right. The reward for these awkward maneuvers was a large room stacked with pool tables lined up like workstations in a factory. Each one had a kelly-green lampshade over it that matched the green felt on the table, and the musty smell of day-old beer hovered over it all.

No one ever came to The Corner Pocket for the elegant ambience, exotic drinks, or sophisticated conversation; that was certain. Yet locals had managed to keep the neon sign lit outside for more than forty years.

She cruised by the bar, hoping to find a parking space. She had to circle the block twice before she found one next to a rusty dumpster. After parking the car, she slipped the keys into her pocket and marched straight ahead, toward the weathered planks and the darkened windows. Although she knew what to expect, a few passersby eyed her strangely as she made her way—alone—into the bar.

She zigged and zagged to get inside, and then stepped onto a layer of sawdust, which carpeted the ground. Every one of the squat oak tables seemed full—amazing for a Wednesday night—so she headed for the bar, where a few spaces still remained. More than once she stepped on a discarded peanut shell and heard it crack under her feet like a seashell on the beach.

Once at the bar, she pulled out a black-bottomed stool and swiveled onto it, not bothering to glance left or right. To be honest, the only company she wanted tonight was a cold beer, a bowl of stale peanuts, and maybe a ghost or two.

Of course, the bartender ignored her, so she busied herself with counting dusty whiskey bottles that sat on a mirrored shelf behind his head. She counted five, including one that rated its own display case, before she moved on to scotch, bourbon, and rum. A glass of something sat next to the cash register, and more than once the bartender took a sip from it when he thought no one was looking.

When she glanced away, her eyes rested on a face in the mirror. A guy sitting two chairs down looked a little younger than she, and she saw a rumpled t-shirt with a pocket on the front. But it wasn't the clothes as much as the way he held his beer bottle that made her pause. He laced his fingers around it, as if the bottle might escape otherwise. Just like Nick used to do. He even looked like Nick, with a shock of brown hair and a burly chest. Rhetta couldn't help but stare. Crazy, wasn't it? Here she'd come to forget and she'd found someone who reminded her exactly of Nick.

"What can I get you?"

The bartender's voice startled her back to reality. "Huh? Oh . . . anything on tap. Make it a light, please."

"Sure thing."

The whole time she kept her gaze locked on the stranger in the mirror. She wanted to speak to him. To see if maybe he sounded like Nick, too. He seemed to be alone, like her, and maybe he'd understand how she felt. But what should she say? Before she could decide, before the bartender returned with her drink, even, the smell of something familiar wafted over to her. Flowers. Flowers mixed with talcum powder. Swirled together into a cheap blend. Like something one would find at a drugstore next to the roll-on deodorant, fluoride toothpaste, and mint dental floss.

"Wanda?" She turned to see Wanda, of all people, standing behind her. Her assistant had changed into a clingy, low-cut dress and had a brightly tattooed butterfly on her right breast. It was something she'd always managed to keep hidden at the office.

"Rhetta. Whadda you doing here?"

"I needed to get out for a while. The service here sucks, but it's close by."

"Do you mind?" Wanda pointed to an empty stool.

"No, go ahead. Good luck getting a drink, though."

Instead of faltering, Wanda brought two of her fingers to her mouth, curved them into an O, and gave a sharp whistle. "Hey, Brad. Over here."

The bartender rushed over to them, carrying a sweating beer bottle in his hand, which he gave to Rhetta.

"Hey, gorgeous," he told Wanda. "What can I do you for?"

"The usual. And don't be so stingy with the scotch this time."

When the bartender retreated, Wanda hopped up onto the stool, which brought the scent of talcum powder, sweet flower petals, and unfiltered cigarettes even closer. She looked pretty tonight, the smell notwithstanding. She'd toned down on her eyeliner and the bar light softened her features.

"Funny, I never knew you come here. Do you play pool?"

Rhetta stifled a laugh. "Hardly. My friend did, though, so he'd drag me along sometimes."

"Oh. Are you talking about the one who passed away?"

She blanched. Although Wanda didn't mean to be cruel, the words stung anyway. "Yeah, the same one. He loved to come here and watch basketball."

Silence lingered between them, so Rhetta took a moment to eye the stranger in the mirror again. "Hey, see that guy in the mirror?" She jerked her head toward the figure by the cash register. He seemed content to nurse his drink rather than talk with anyone else. "It's uncanny how much that guy looks like my friend. Isn't that something?"

"Really? Do you have a picture I could see?"

"Sure." Rhetta pulled out a key ring, which had a few pictures framed in scratched plastic between her car and apartment keys. Her favorite, the one she never showed anyone because they might wonder why in the world she would keep a picture of a married man on her key ring, showed her and Nick on the beach, sitting between lifeguard towers four and five, as always. "Here he is. It's old, but you'll get the idea."

Wanda studied the picture. She seemed to be looking for something, but it was hard to tell what. Finally, she handed the key ring back. "I don't see it."

"What do mean? It looks exactly like him. Look at that hair. And those muscles. C'mon. You've got to be kidding." Rhetta shoved the key ring back toward Wanda.

"Sorry, Rhetta. I don't see it at all." Wanda looked apologetic, but certain. "That guy's hair is way too blond. They don't look anything alike."

Why would she say that? Rhetta withdrew the picture, her enthusiasm ebbing. "I don't know. I still think it looks like him. Maybe I'll go say something."

The bartender reappeared then, holding a glass of gold liquid, which he placed on the bar in front of Wanda. "Here you go, gorgeous. On the house."

"Thanks, Brad."

"So what do you think? Dare me to strike up a conversation?"

Finally, Wanda turned to face her. "Don't do it."

"Why not? It couldn't hurt, and he might be flattered."

"I don't know how to tell you this, but that guy looks nothing like your friend. At least, not in the picture."

"What? No, you're wrong. He has the same build, the same facial structure. And look, he even holds his beer the same way. He's a dead ringer, I'm telling you."

"Rhetta—"

"What's wrong with you?" She didn't mean to snap, but why couldn't Wanda see it, too?

"Didn't your friend have dark hair?" Wanda asked. "That guy's hair is almost blond." Her voice sounded too kind now, and too patient. As if Rhetta were a child who needed to be pacified.

"Okay, but you didn't know Nick. He always held his beer like that. Always."

"Look around you, Rhetta. Half the guys in here hold their beer like that."

"Oh. Well, you didn't know him well enough to see what I see."

"Let me level with you." Wanda took a slow drink from her glass, which looked like it could have come from one of the scotch bottles on the shelf. Straight up, too, if the dark color was any indication. "I know that guy. You don't want to talk to him."

"You do?" Funny how the more Wanda spoke, the sharper the details in the mirror became. Maybe the guy's hair was a shade too light. Not thick enough, either. And what was with the scar that ran from one eye to his temple? Granted, it was faint, but it was on the wrong side. Nick's scar ran across his forward above his left eye, not his right. Even the man's neck seemed too thick for his t-shirt now, the way it bulged over the top like that. "Maybe you're right."

"I *am* right. But I understand. You miss your friend."

"It looks a *little* like him."

"Don't beat yourself up. I did that all the time when my dad passed away. Any guy I saw over sixty I would swear was his twin. It'll go away. You need some time, is all."

"Great. Now I'm turning into a stalker."

"You're not a stalker. It's perfectly normal. Weird, but normal."

"Guess I can live with weird." Rhetta reached for her beer, which had gradually warmed. "You know, I never told you thanks for calling me last night. Tracking me down. I appreciate it."

"Well, that's the thing. At first I didn't know what to do. I didn't want to interrupt you, but I thought you should know."

"Well, your instinct was right. I *did* want to know."

"People don't disappear from the hospital's system like that for no reason." She sipped again from her drink before continuing. "When a patient dies, the information in a hospital directory stays there for a few days. There's a space for something called 'general condition,' and it's only one word. Could be undetermined, good, fair, serious, or critical." Wanda paused to run her finger around the lip of her glass, lost in thought. "But that changes when someone dies. Then it shows up as 'deceased.' Nothing more and nothing less. I used to be able to tell people when they specifically asked for a patient by name. That's all I could say."

"Ouch. That must have been hard if the caller didn't know."

"You got that right. One time I told someone that a patient in pediatrics was deceased. It was horrible. I could hear the wailing even when I pulled the phone away from my ear."

"So, what do you think happened with Nick? Why would someone take away his record? It seems so simple. It doesn't say how he died, right?"

"Nope, only that he died." Wanda once more lifted the drink to her lips. At this pace she'd be done before Rhetta even took a second pull on her beer. "Unless someone didn't want the media to know. See, the information desk is allowed to tell other people, like newspaper reporters, if a patient dies, and maybe whoever deleted the record didn't want it to become public."

Interesting. Nick was a cop, after all, and reporters loved to cover stories about cops. Maybe the person who deleted the record knew that. Or maybe not. "You think they did it to protect themselves?"

"My bet is they wanted more time. Don't know for sure, but that's my guess. Say, all of this talk about death is depressing me. I'm sorry about your friend, but can we talk about something else for a while?"

"I guess." Funny how it didn't strike Rhetta the same way. It seemed normal. She'd been under a cloud for so long it didn't seem unusual to talk about death and dying. Maybe coming to The Corner Pocket wasn't such a good idea, after all.

"Look, Wanda, I'm kind of tired." Now that her illusion was

shattered, she felt drained. "I think I'll go home. You okay by yourself?"

"But I'm not by myself." Wanda gestured at the bartender, who hovered nearby. "I've got plenty of company. See you Monday."

Rhetta withdrew a five-dollar bill from her pocket and rose. When she slapped it on the counter, she noticed the mysterious figure sitting two doors down was watching her in the mirror, too. Wanda was right. He and Nick looked nothing alike, after all.

A few mornings later, Rhetta slept later than usual, long after the garbage truck had come and gone through the alley behind her apartment. So late, in fact, that sunlight flooded her bedroom and made turning on a light unnecessary when she arose.

Groggily she padded toward the front door and opened it a crack to pull in the morning newspaper.

Once she scooted in the newspaper, she walked into the kitchen and laid it on the table. Unlike tomorrow's edition, which would weigh close to two pounds when stuffed with coupons and help-wanted ads, the Saturday edition looked positively svelte. She found the local news section in no time, where a headline about the local police department called out for her attention.

Seems the timesheet investigation continued, with Officer Larry Belknap still named as one of five suspects. Considering the matter "administrative," the department declined to place the officers on leave, the article said, and allowed them to keep their guns, their paychecks, and their dignity for the time being.

When she finished reading, the telephone rang. She thought about ignoring it, but what else did she have going on? So she lifted the receiver and mentally prepared to say no to whatever telemarketer had dialed her.

"Rhetta?"

Expected or not, she brightened at the sound of Eamon's voice. "Good morning."

"Guess you haven't been out for a while."

"Guilty. I took a few days off from work. As a matter of fact, you're the first person I've talked to."

"Well, I didn't want to wake you. You doing okay?"

He sounded cautious. She wasn't used to that. Normally, he'd launch right into whatever he had to say. "Yeah, I'm okay. Still feel kind of wobbly, though. Bad news does that to me."

"I know what you mean. Can't get your sea legs, right?"

At the mention of his boat, her mood lightened a bit. He'd be standing by the teak bar, if she had to guess, or maybe leaning over the stove in the galley, or opening the cabinet door with one push of his thumb. Whatever he was doing, she wished she could see him face-to-face to know for sure. "You on the boat?"

"Oh, yeah. It would be nice to have some company, though."

Much as she wanted to climb through the telephone and join him, she'd done nothing more than sleep over the past few days. A pile of mail sat on her countertop, and heaven only knew how many dirty clothes she'd blindly tossed into the laundry basket. "Please don't ask me to come over there right now."

"Why not?"

"Because I'll say yes, and then I won't be able to pay my rent, or the phone bill, or—"

"Okay, I get it. I have to make do with hearing your voice. I can live with that."

She brought the telephone closer to her ear. No matter what had happened over the course of Nick's illness, she would never regret meeting Dr. Eamon McAllister. It was the one thing that had made the past week bearable.

"I thought I saw Nick sitting in a bar around here. Is that weird?" The moment she threw out the question, she wanted to pull it back in again. If she didn't stop talking about Nick, then Eamon would think he had no chance with her. And that was definitely not the case. "I mean, I could tell after a while the guy looked nothing like him. Maybe my head's a little messed up because Nick and I were such good friends." She stressed the word "friends" on purpose, hoping he'd take the hint.

"Is that all you two were?" He sounded serious now, his voice deeper.

"Trust me, we were a lot better friends than anything else."

"So you never slept with him?"

The question stopped her cold. Torn between wanting to answer immediately and wondering why in the world he would ask something like that, she said nothing.

"Rhetta?"

"Still here." For some reason, she couldn't think of anything glib or funny to say. He had no right to ask her a question like that in the middle of a Saturday morning just a few days after she learned about Nick's death. No right at all. But the fact that he'd posed the question must be a good sign, right? Why should he care if they'd slept together? He wouldn't care if she meant nothing at all to him, or if she was no more than a lunch partner or a dinner date that he had no intention of keeping in his life.

"Well?"

"I don't know what to tell you, Eamon. It's really none of your business."

"Oh, I get it."

"No, it's not what you think. We did sleep together, but only once. It was a long time ago and it was a big mistake."

"I see." Though from the tone of his voice she could tell he didn't understand at all.

"Disappointed?"

"No, you're a grown woman, Rhetta. And you're right. It's none of my business. Forget I asked."

Which was much easier said than done. "If you want to talk about it, I will. I mean, if it's bothering you."

He sighed into the telephone, purposefully buying time. "No, really. Forget I asked. Hey, I know what I can do to make up for being such an idiot. Since you won't come here, and I'm guessing you don't want me to go there . . ."

Suddenly he cleared his throat and began to sing. Softly at first, but then with more confidence when he realized she wasn't going to interrupt him.

Sweet comic valentine . . .

Of course. The song broadcast over the hospital's intercom for all to hear. Drunk or not, the neonatologist had crooned those very words to a special pediatric nurse. Eamon's version sounded so much better, and so much more appropriate, there in the privacy of her kitchen on a sleepy Saturday morning.

"Bravo, Doctor." She placed the phone between her chin and her shoulder to free up her hands so she could clap once he'd finished. "Encore. Encore."

"Oh, no. You don't get any more until you see me in person."

"Well, that won't be too long from now. You're going with me to the funeral, right?"

"Better than that. You promised me dinner some time."

"Oh yeah, about that. Do you mind if we push that back? I've got a million things to do around here and only one day to do them. Would you mind?"

"No, I understand. I have someone I need to meet with anyway. And I still get to see you first thing on Monday, right?"

"Definitely. Thanks, Eamon. I'll see you then."

"Good-bye, funny valentine."

CHAPTER 14

She didn't own any black clothes. After spending the rest of the weekend wandering around the apartment, finally Monday morning arrived. Rhetta stood in front of her bedroom closet and blindly riffled through the rack of blouses, pants, and skirts.

Sunlight poured through the bedroom window, which didn't seem quite right. Why wasn't the weather bleak and anxious, to match her mood? She had awoken mad at the world. At the hospital, because they couldn't do more to save Nick. At Beryl, because she didn't know or care enough to plan a decent funeral. At the weather, even. Finally, she picked out a charcoal gray skirt and navy blouse, which would have to do. Not that it mattered, but somehow it seemed wrong to wear anything bright or cheerful on this day of all days.

She left the apartment when Eamon honked outside. She really didn't need to hurry, though, because nothing would alter the outcome. They could drive ninety miles an hour down the freeway, and Nick still would be lowered into a dank hole after oh-eight-hundred hours. Nothing would ever change that.

But the rest of the city didn't seem to care. A city bus rumbled in the distance, a recycling truck whined as it turned onto her street, and nearer yet, a family of blue jays chatted. It was only another day. Nothing different, nothing special, only one more Monday in a whole line of Mondays.

After driving down a few side streets, Eamon maneuvered the car onto a palm-lined drive. They were almost at St. Stephen's.

An unbroken line of cars stretched along both sides of the boulevard, continuing for at least half a mile. Nearer the church, a row of shiny police motorcycles stood in silent tribute.

"Do you think there's a mistake?" she yelled over the rush of air. It didn't seem possible that *so* many people had heard about Nick's funeral.

"I don't think so. Geez," he shouted back, "look at this crowd."

They cruised by the church's entrance. Hundreds of people milled on the steps. Some of them wore full-dress police uniforms, complete with brass buttons on their shoulder seams and holsters at their hips. The women, meanwhile, wore dark hats angled against the morning sun, like a flock of crows nesting on polished stone. "I can't believe it."

"We'll be lucky to find a parking place." They drove down the street and finally turned onto another lane, which had a few gaps by its curb. As soon as they squeezed into an empty space, one of the few, Rhetta flung open the convertible's door and began to walk toward the gathering, which seemed to grow with each step. Now people were forced backward as others joined them, onto the sidewalk, in a pool of dark fabric. She allowed Eamon to cross in front of her, and he cut them a path through the shifting crowd.

They angled through the marble archway and landed in the church's anteroom. Sunlight pierced stained-glass windows above and cast bolts of ruby red, marine blue, golden yellow, and clover green below. While she waited her turn to sign a guest book, she studied colorful pictures of Nick placed around the narthex. Nick in his formal police dress uniform; Nick wearing a slanted mortarboard, graduating from Cal West; a young Nick in a basketball jersey, with a big grin on his face. Time stalled in the pictures, and his eyes, his smile, which was broad, even the tilt of his head, hadn't changed through all of the years. From scruffy little boy to barely-enough-credits-to-graduate college student, he was, unmistakably, Nick.

Unable to breathe, Rhetta stepped away from the line and gratefully followed Eamon into the sanctuary. Seats already were scarce, and they were forced to sit in the last row. The pew felt as hard and stoic as the faces around her. No one dared smile, so they squirmed and fidgeted and thumbed through the hymnals in front of them—looking for what?—instead.

Finally, a robed man inched down the center aisle. With the priest's entrance, the organist began to play a hymn. Given the drama of the moment, she almost expected the organist to leap up and make a dramatic announcement. Praise the Lord, by some miracle of miracles, Nick wasn't really dead. They could all go home now. But that didn't happen, of course. The door swung shut behind the Father, and when it reopened, there was Beryl, wearing a polka-dot dress Rhetta had never seen before. She marched straight down the center aisle and her French braid changed colors as she passed under the sun's reflection in the stained glass: reddish one moment and gold the next, and then it turned shadowy auburn when she walked under the Garden of Gethsemane.

All in all, the memorial service was extremely short. In no time at all, the priest invited them to say the Lord's Prayer, which she knew by heart. She had memorized the words from a sympathy card an aunt once had given to her.

". . . and the power, and the glory, forever. Amen."

"Amen." Eamon must have been anxious to leave the church, too, because he took her hand once they rose, and wove them through the crowd like a pro. She'd read one of the bulletins while waiting for the service to begin—there was nothing else to do—which announced the church would hold a reception in the recreation hall afterward.

There would be no formal burial, the bulletin announced, in

deference to the deceased wife's wishes. In deference to *Beryl's* wishes. Nick's body would be cremated, not buried, and his ashes later scattered over the Pacific Ocean. It was poetic, really. Not what he had wanted, but more like Rhetta's plan. He'd wanted a wake when his time came, with a saxophone solo and friends half-drunk on whiskey, but apparently he wouldn't be getting his wish. It was amazing the Catholic Church even allowed for the cremation.

She and Eamon made a beeline for a modest stucco building once they left the service. A warm breeze wafted over the asphalt in the parking lot, stirring up puffs of dust between the cars.

Compared to the ornate church, the recreation hall was nothing special: a one-story building, shaped like a triangle, with an A-frame roof. They entered a whirlwind of activity once they came up the steps. A gaggle of older women rushed about, carrying Jell-O cubes in clear dishes, silver trays piled with tea sandwiches, and indistinguishable casseroles in ceramic pots. One of the women placed a tray of croissants on a folding table, while another filled an enormous steel coffeepot with tap water. The woman at the coffee urn shot Rhetta a look that said she was none too happy to have her and Eamon appear so soon. Charity was one thing, her eyes seemed to say, but there were procedures to be followed, and they were not welcome yet.

Close on the heels of the matriarchs twirled a young girl, freshly scrubbed, with bare legs, who had been entrusted mainly with paper plates and plastic cutlery. The women spoke to the girl in shorthand, using one-word commands—"garnish!" "creamer!" "ladle!"—and they threw the words over their shoulders as they trekked to and from the kitchen.

Six-foot-long folding tables, row after row of them, stretched from one side of the hall to the other. Red, white, and blue bunting capped each of the tables' ends, and the paper had been twisted into rosettes of swirled color.

The room must have pulled double, or even triple, duty, because the back, paneled wall was niched with pass-throughs from the kitchen to the eating area. No doubt it was used for everything from wedding receptions to potlucks to rousing games of bingo. Orange tape even marked the floor under their feet for the out-of-bounds line of a basketball court. No wonder the air was a mishmash of liniment and rubber soles, stale coffee grounds and fried eggs, plus an overarching hint of bleach that topped it all off.

She and Eamon hovered near the open door until Beryl entered the room, accompanied by a police officer. Beryl stood awkwardly with her back against the wood-paneled wall, barely speaking to her companion, until one of the church ladies approached her. The woman balanced on her toes to whisper something into Beryl's ear, and then gestured to the first table, which was placed next to the empty stage.

"Let's go say something," Rhetta said. She led Eamon down a wide swath left between the folding tables, to where Beryl stood. "Are you all right?" The woman looked drained from this close up, as if her calm façade would crack at the first wrong word.

"I guess so." Beryl waited until the church woman turned away before grabbing Rhetta's arm. "I sure could use a cigarette."

"Sorry, I don't have any. Let's get out of here." There wasn't anywhere to go, though. The crowd had begun to file into the social hall, and Beryl's escort blocked the back exit, whether he meant to or not. They were stuck—sandwiched between the approaching hordes and a policeman—with nowhere to turn.

"This will have to do." Rhetta pulled out a clunky folding chair for Beryl. "Can I get you anything?"

"No, thanks. I want today to be over with. People keep staring at me."

A small crowd had gathered behind them, and sure enough, everyone was eyeing the young widow like tourists ogling an exotic newborn at the zoo. Their eyes were ablaze with pure, unadulterated curiosity.

Beryl nervously smoothed a crease on the front of her dress. "I didn't even have anything new to wear. I had to go shopping yesterday to get this."

Oh. How efficient of her. That Beryl would stop at a department store the day before her husband's funeral, and be coherent enough to plow through racks of dresses. That she could pick and choose among styles, designers, price tags—shades of black, even—in an artificial light, when only a few days before, she'd been at the hospital signing Nick's death certificate. Did Beryl unlace the high-top tennis shoes from Nick's feet once the ventilator shut down? What did she say to him? Was he even awake to hear her? His dying moments should have left her too drained to do much of anything, but this was Beryl, after all, and she was practical if nothing else. Practical enough to buy clothes the day before her husband's funeral.

Eamon knelt by the widow's chair. "How're you holding up?" He didn't know her well enough to say more.

"Okay, I guess."

"We all feel terrible about what happened. It was such a stupid accident."

"I know that. You don't have a cigarette, do you?"

He looked at her sideways. "Nope, no cigarettes. Why don't you have a bite to eat?"

"Sure. Okay."

Eamon tried to stand, but the crowd had grown so thick around them he was stuck in a crouch, bent forward, with his hands on his knees. "They've got me trapped."

"Here, let me." Rhetta scanned the room and spotted the elderly woman with the croissants, who now presided over a folding table. The lady amicably chatted with each person in line as she doled out food. After a short pause, Rhetta made her way through the crowd toward the woman. The table held a plate of croissants, a few covered casserole dishes, some salad, and a crystal jar with some funny-looking sauce in it.

"Fig with tapenade?" the woman asked.

"Excuse me?" Where were the pigs-in-a-blanket, the ever-present miniature quiches, the hard rolls with butter, or at least something she could identify? She didn't expect to see the woman open one of the casserole dishes and show her a fig sliced open and stuffed with oily meat.

"It's from a recipe in one of my magazines," the woman answered, her voice a little chilled now. "It's figs with anchovies and olives. Don't you think it's pretty?"

Olive oil glimmered on the fish meat. "I guess so."

The woman took great pains to scoop a fig from the casserole dish and center it on a plate, which she gave to Rhetta. "Looks like it did in the picture. You're going to love it." She winked, too, as if to convince her.

"Thanks. Can I have a plain croissant?"

"I suppose." The lady grudgingly added a croissant to the plate she'd so carefully arranged.

Rhetta accepted the food, and began to make her way back to where Beryl sat, which was no easy trick considering the depth of the crowd. It took her almost a full minute to navigate her way back to Beryl's side.

"Okay, I give. What *is* that?" Beryl eyed the plate suspiciously.

"Anchovies with something. It's from a magazine. The lady seemed really proud of it." Gingerly, she placed the plate in Beryl's lap. "Said it looks like the picture."

Beryl crinkled her nose. "I stopped eating fish a long time ago." She lifted the plate, and resolutely set it on the ground, under her chair. "Nick was allergic to iodine. Severely allergic."

She'd spoken so quietly, Rhetta wasn't convinced she'd heard her correctly. "Excuse me?"

The flurry around them seemed to dim. Rhetta remembered the last time she'd spoken to anyone about Nick. It was in the lobby of the ICU. The pharmacist read his shorthand notes and marveled that Nick had gotten almost two hundred fifty microcuries of iodine from a hospital before the thyroid test. That would be a problem, he'd said, if you give that much to someone who's allergic.

By the time the memory faded, a stranger had sandwiched himself between her and Beryl. Even if she could find her voice, what would she say? Nothing made sense at the moment.

"Beryl?" But her friend didn't seem to be able to hear her; the man in between had closed off the space completely. There was nothing she could do but watch the young widow disappear from view.

Rhetta stumbled into a table placed directly behind her and reached for a folding chair at the last second. Voices droned—the whine of children, polite laughter, the gurgle of a coffeepot—but the sounds mixed together, creating one giant, barely distinguishable hum.

She clearly remembered seeing Andrew hunch over his notes in the ICU lobby, his eyes glued to them. He'd been searching for something. And when he found it—the root of Nick's allergies—he'd whistled softly under his breath.

Chapter 15

After feigning interest in the reception for a while, Rhetta suddenly developed a splitting headache and asked Eamon to drive her home.

He kissed her on the cheek when they arrived at her apartment, and then joked about the rain check she'd offered him for dinner.

What? She had so many other things to think about that dinner seemed to be the least of her worries. So she mumbled something or other that seemed to do the trick, because he left her alone on the stoop and retreated to his car. She watched as the taillights dimmed. Once they disappeared completely, she turned and walked to her own car, which was parked at the curb, and slid behind the steering wheel.

She drove to the freeway in a fog, so distracted she almost missed her turnoff a few minutes later. At the last second, she jerked the steering wheel hard to the right, which caused a driver behind her to lay on his horn and the cacophony followed her onto the off-ramp. Up ahead sat the familiar dirt-brown medical center; a concrete island in a sea of asphalt. If she parked in the hospital's main lot, she reasoned, it would take only a minute or two to reach the pharmacy department.

Once parked, she hurried under the porte cochere and dashed through the sliding-glass door that led to the main lobby. Midday sun blanched the sofas and chairs in the waiting room pale, turning everything to the color of mush. Faces sped by in a blur—a harried parent, someone in white clutching a clipboard, an elderly volunteer wheeling a cart of books. What if Andrew wasn't even in his office? It was still lunchtime, after all, and he could be almost anywhere in the medical center.

When she finally reached the pharmacy department, a plump woman with enormous rhinestone earrings greeted her. "May I help you?"

"I need to see Andrew Wong."

"Really?" The receptionist picked at an earring distractedly.

"Yes, if you don't mind." It was obviously time for some serious kissing-up. "By the way, I love your earrings."

The receptionist giggled, and then pointed to a molded plastic chair. "Thank you kindly. Name's Crystal. Have a seat."

Before she sat down, Rhetta glanced at a bookcase that stood next to the chair. She saw dog-eared copies of a pharmacy magazine, some paperback textbooks, and the familiar cobalt-blue doctors' reference guide. In the middle of the shelf, a thinner book—which had the ominous word *Poisons* stamped on its spine—balanced precariously. She pried the book from the lineup, perched on a chair, and turned to the table of contents. Immediately, she spotted a section titled "Iodine and Its Compounds," and softly read the opening sentence aloud. *The corrosive action of iodine may lead to circulatory collapse. With aspiration, the result is bronchopneumonia, a chief cause of death when it occurs.*

When it occurs. Nick had lain so still in his hospital bed, connected to tubes and wires and contraptions that buzzed and whirred. Somehow, she'd known he would never leave the hospital alive.

"Hi, Rhetta." Just then, Andrew Wong loped around a corner.

Quickly, she slipped the book back into its place and jumped to her feet. "Andrew." The receptionist stared at them, all the while twirling the sparkly earring, but Rhetta ignored her. "Have you had lunch yet?"

"Well, no. I haven't."

"Good." It was time for her to take a look at Nick's electronic medical record—something the staff called an EMR—no matter what the pharmacist or the nurses, or even a curious receptionist named Crystal, thought.

She worked quickly, before he had a chance to protest, by taking his hand and leading him away from the receptionist's desk. When they reached the lobby, she angled her body sideways to shield them from a river of people. "I have to ask you something first. What I really need is a favor."

"A favor?" He stared at her blankly. "What kind of favor?"

"I need to see a medical record." He started to shake his head, but her voice hardened. "Before you say no, you need to understand why I'm asking." Now, how could she explain this without sounding insane? Murder, conspiracy, poisoning—that stuff happened only on the nightly news, and it only happened to other people. It didn't happen under the bright lights of a hospital, for goodness sake, and it didn't happen to a cop like Nick. She stepped closer to the pharmacist.

"I have my doubts about Nick Tahari's death," she whispered. "You said that when they scan at other hospitals, they don't use the same dosage St. James does. I know you think something's wrong." She was taking a huge gamble, spilling her thoughts like this, but every instinct told her it was the right thing to do. "This morning his wife told me Nick was allergic to iodine."

The pharmacist's eyes widened. He didn't say anything for a moment, and when he finally did, it was in a whisper, too. "Well, now that you mention it, a lot of things don't add up. Like, why would someone pick now to hack into the EMR database?"

"What do you mean, someone hacked into the EMRs?"

"Someone broke into the medical records department last night and accessed the database. My roommate works there, and he said everyone's talking about it."

"How'd they know it'd been hacked?"

"Nothing too sophisticated. The person forgot to log off when he was through. He—or she—got in using a general code."

"What if it was Nick's chart he was after?"

"There's no way to tell."

She looked at him askance. "Of course there is. We could go there now. I'm sure your roommate can find out."

"I don't know, Rhetta." The pharmacist crinkled his nose as if the very idea smelled bad to him.

"C'mon, Andrew. You said yourself some things don't add up. Here's our chance to find out."

"I'll tell you what. I'll take you there. But if Chad's gone, we've gotta turn back. I can't get caught compromising a patient's privacy."

While it pained her to state the obvious, it seemed Andrew must have forgotten one tiny detail. "Nick died, Andrew. How can we invade his privacy now?"

"Most patient privacy laws protect you for at least ten years. But who knows. Maybe his record's in perfect shape. I only hope Chad's there."

They skirted around the information desk and headed for the medical records department. As one of the few places in the hospital to get foot traffic—people dropped by constantly to pick up medical records, photocopy something for their insurance company, or return forms—it enjoyed easy access to the lobby. And because the public had access, there was no need to swipe an identification badge or punch in a code. Andrew opened the door for her once they arrived, and it swung shut behind them.

The room looked bland enough. Tall, putty-colored filing cabinets rose floor to ceiling in the reception area. About the only splash of color came from a stack of brochures—"Know

Your Rights," the cover said—piled on the counter.

They waited patiently until an older woman with stooped shoulders appeared. She seemed to know Andrew, because she smiled.

"Hi, Andy. Haven't seen you in a dog's age. Looking for Chad?"

"Sure am, Gladys." He sounded noticeably relieved. "Good to see you're still working here."

"They can't get rid of me yet." Her eyes twinkled when she spoke. For all anyone knew, this spry woman could have been at the hospital fifty years ago when they first opened the place. Easy to imagine she'd strolled the halls long before any of them had been born. "Let me get him for you. Wish I could stay and chat, but I'm late for my lunch break."

She shuffled back to one of the cubicles on the end. A second later, a young African-American popped his head over the top of the partition. "Hey, Andy. What's up?" He didn't look surprised to see him, just curious. Especially when he noticed Rhetta standing by Andrew's side.

"Hey, Chad, this is Rhetta. She works up in the PR department."

"Oh yeah?" That lured him out of the cubicle, and he walked around the partition to meet them. "Do you write ads and stuff for the hospital?"

Since now wasn't the best time to provide a tutorial on public relations, Rhetta opted to keep her answer short and sweet. "No, that's our ad agency. We do stuff like press releases, video news clips, media conferences. That kind of thing."

Of course, nothing she'd said had anything to do with medical records, and he looked a little puzzled.

"Okay, so what's up? You guys come over here to buy me lunch?"

"You wish," Andrew said. "We need a favor."

The word "favor" dredged a memory from Rhetta's consciousness of the week before. She'd said the exact same words to Wanda when she wanted to know about Nick. While that exchange hadn't turned out particularly well—someone had restricted Nick's admitting information—at least Wanda had only asked for chocolate for her trouble. Hopefully, this guy would be just as easy to placate.

Chad waved them behind the counter, and they followed him to the back of the room. Unlike most of the cubicles, his desk overlooked a large window and bright noon sun spilled through the glass and landed on an unopened box of tissues.

"Wow. I've never seen such a clean desk before," she said.

"Welcome to my home." Chad gestured grandly. "Everything's computerized now. The doctors all work off templates. So, what's going on?"

He plopped into a chair and stared up at her.

Now, where to begin? How could she possibly explain to a stranger why she needed to see Nick's electronic medical record without sounding like a total lunatic? Odds were good she couldn't, so she might as well jump right in. "Andrew told me you guys got hacked into last night."

"Yep. Someone accessed the system, all right. We didn't find out about it until we all showed up for work this morning. Whoever did it wasn't too bright, 'cuz they forgot to log out."

"Forgot? Or maybe they were scared off," Andrew said.

Why, Rhetta hadn't even thought of that. Maybe he was right. It could have been a security guard who scared the culprit away.

"Good thinking, Andrew. Maybe someone showed up so they had to leave in a hurry."

"Did you figure out what the hacker wanted, Chad?"

"Honestly?" He looked at them sheepishly. "There's no way to tell unless we go through every medical record. They could have printed something, sent a file to another computer, deleted a record. There's no way to tell. We emailed all of our record-holders for the past year and let 'em know their social security numbers might be compromised, but that's about all we can do."

"Maybe." Slowly, Rhetta sat down on a corner of the desk. "What if we told you that we're concerned about a certain medical record? A very special medical record."

"I'd say you have my attention. Go on."

Now came the tricky part. She took a deep breath. "A little over a week ago, a police officer was admitted to our ICU." No need to name names. For all this guy Chad knew, it was a random officer with a random injury. "He died last week."

"That sucks. But why would someone want to mess with his EMR?"

"Good question," Andrew said. "Usually I know why someone's in my unit and the treatment plan makes total sense. But not this time."

"Now I'm confused. You didn't agree with the guy's diagnosis, or you didn't agree with how he was treated?"

"Both." Andrew paused dramatically to let the words sink in. "Here we have a healthy, thirty-year-old cop who got a test he shouldn't have gotten. Call him 'patient x.' The test puts him in our hospital, where he goes into respiratory distress and dies."

Put like that, they *could* have been discussing anyone. Even though she'd first decided against naming names, now it seemed wrong. Nick was so much more than a random patient and so much more than the letter "x."

"His name was Nick Tahari," she said. "He died after only a few days in our ICU. It wasn't an accident."

"Let me get this straight." Chad looked more confused than ever. "You want to take a look at this guy's records, to see if maybe something's been changed?"

"Missing, changed, whatever."

"As long as you know the patient's name and date of admission, *and* you have a credible reason for wanting the information, I think I can help you."

Thank goodness. Rhetta's shoulders finally began to untense. "We really appreciate this."

"Course, it's all protected information, so we need to notify his next-of-kin first."

Apparently she'd let her guard down too soon. "To be honest," she said, her shoulders beginning to tense again, "we can't let that happen. She's the one we're worried about."

"Huh?"

By now Rhetta wanted to throw up her hands. Every second they spent explaining things to Chad was one less second they had to figure this out. "Look, we don't have a lot of time. Are you going to help us or not?"

"Whoa. Slow down. I didn't say I wouldn't help you. I only wanted to know why."

"Sorry. Guess I'm a little tense."

"She was a friend of the patient's," Andrew explained. "A very good friend."

"Okay. All I need to know," Chad said. "First things first. Spell his name."

He pulled the computer keyboard close and began to type letters as Rhetta called them out. When he was through, he typed something else at the top of the screen, and a record appeared. Instinctively, she leaned in.

"Here we go. Looks like the record's all here." Chad scrolled down the pages, glancing at each one as he went. "The notes aren't that thorough, but I've seen worse."

"Does anything look different? Out of place?"

"Be patient."

She was pushing hard; she knew that, so she forced herself to shut up and let this guy do his job. No need to irritate him.

After a second, Chad pointed at some tabs that lined the top of the record. "Here's what you want. It'll tell us whether a record was deleted or not."

He clicked on a tab that read "recover deleted notes." As if by magic, a new screen appeared that was filled with writing and an elaborate signature.

"What does it mean?" Incredible that an entire page could pop up out of thin air.

"It's a consent to treat," Andrew said somberly. "It tells the technician if there's any reason a patient shouldn't have a test. They scan it into the notes later. Look right here. That looks like a woman's signature."

Rhetta immediately recognized the elaborate capital letters in Beryl's name. Equally troubling was a strange acronym she'd written above it. "I don't get it. What does 'NKA' stand for?"

"Even I know that one," Chad said. To be honest, since he'd fallen quiet, she almost forgot he was there. "It means the patient has no known allergies."

"He's right, Rhetta." Andrew looked shell-shocked. "Let's close out of the record, quick. That's what we needed to see."

When Chad moved forward, she reached out to stop him. "Don't. We'll need that record. Can you print it out for me?"

"I guess so. Andrew, what do you make of it? Do you think it was her who came in over the weekend and tried to delete the record?"

"Oh, yeah. I'd bet my life on it."

Interesting choice of words, Rhetta thought, as finally she looked away. Now that they had what they came for, why did she feel like yanking the plug on the computer and letting the screen fade to black? Letting the initials seep back into the ether, where they belonged and where they wouldn't raise more questions. Letting everything get back to normal. She knew Beryl was smart—the woman was a coronary care nurse, for goodness sakes—but she had no idea how smart. Or how cunning. If she was willing to hack into a computer to alter Nick's record, what else would she do?

Rhetta waited for Chad to print out the form, her eyes darting from the printer to the window and then back again. Traffic had slowed outside, which meant lunchtime was almost over.

Walking out of the medical records department alone, a photocopied page from Nick's EMR safely tucked under her arm, Rhetta moved through the lobby single-mindedly. The sooner she got Nick's record to her own office, the better, so she quickened her pace even more.

Maybe that's why she didn't notice a colorful object that lay on the ground, until her foot kicked against it. It was a child's book, of all things, face up on the carpet. Probably an escapee from the volunteer's book cart earlier. The one that was now parked half in and half out of the hospital's gift shop. When she bent to examine it, Nick's medical record slipped out from under her arm and sailed to the ground. A hand reached out to grab it before she could move; before she could do anything more than stare.

"This yours?"

She glanced up to see Carlos Cervantes, Nick's old fraternity brother. Once again she noticed the bloodshot eyes, more red than white, and the way his skin had yellowed. He wore a white lab coat.

"Yes, it's mine. Give it to me."

He waved it in front of her like a child playing keep-away. "Maybe," he taunted. "Say please first."

Clenching her teeth, Rhetta spoke again. "*Please* give that to me."

"That's better." With a smirk, he handed over the precious piece of paper. He also kicked the book aside, and it sailed back in the direction of the gift shop.

"Oh, great, now someone else can trip on it," she said. She turned away from him and followed it, until the book came to rest in front of the cash register. The minute she entered the gift shop, she smelled the stretched plastic of a bundle of balloons that floated overhead.

As she expected, the store was crammed full of balloons, pastel-colored knickknacks, and children's books. She bent down to scoop up the one that lay on the ground.

"Jeez, you're picky." Carlos's voice sounded from somewhere behind her. "Say, do you have a second?"

"Huh?" She rose with the book in her hand. Whatever would Carlos want to say to her? The first time she saw him, a few days back in the parking lot by the surgery suites, he seemed so happy about Nick's diagnosis, it was no wonder she didn't like him. Or like sharing the same cramped space with him now.

"Here, I'll put that away." He plucked the book from her hand before she could protest—my, but he was quick—and dropped it into the overflowing book cart.

"Thanks, I guess. Wow, look at all of those books," she marveled. Nick would have had a field day if he were with them. He always loved cartoons and comic books and other things that normally only children like.

"You didn't let me finish the other day." Carlos's voice brought her back to reality.

"You mean that time we were out there in the parking lot? With all the smokers? I seem to recall you walked away first, not me."

"Yeah, well. I guess I didn't want to talk to you in front of an audience."

"Look, Carlos. Do you need something? I'm in a hurry." She became aware again of the photocopied EMR wedged—more firmly, now—under her arm.

"I wanted to tell you something out there. But we don't really know each other."

"That's true. Guess the only thing we have in common is Nick. And we both work here."

"You know Nick wasn't the reason I got kicked out of school, right? That's not why I ended up here. Like this." He pointed to his lab coat, where she noticed for the first time the frayed buttonholes, limp fabric, and a ragged hem.

"Pardon me?" Why would Carlos bring that up now? Here, in a cramped gift shop with the smell of fresh plastic encircling them.

"Nick wasn't the reason I left Cal West. To be honest, he saved me."

"What do you mean, he saved you? We all thought getting kicked out of school was the worst thing that ever happened to you. You said you hated Nick for it."

"That was for show. I've told that lie so many times, sometimes I forget what really happened."

"So what's the truth?"

"I flunked out of school. Nick gave me the perfect excuse to save face. All of this time people thought he was the reason I left. I always meant to thank him for that, but I never got the chance."

"But you were there the night they admitted Nick." She clearly remembered standing on hot asphalt and listening to Carlos tell her he wouldn't help Nick when they brought him in.

"Pfffttt. All for show. I wanted the nurses to think I'm a big deal and docs call on me when they need help. To be honest, I didn't even see Nick that night. They whisked him in and out of triage so fast I didn't know he was there."

Well, if that didn't beat all. Here she thought Carlos could have played a role in Nick's death, only to find out his whole story was a lie. Nick had given him an excuse so he didn't have to admit he'd flunked out of college.

"What about the suicide attempt? Everyone said you threw yourself off the pier."

"Yeah, well, that's a funny story." His sour expression told her he didn't actually find it the least bit funny. "I didn't jump. I fell off. Does that suck, or what? I even knew the surfer who 'saved' me. Guess it's not a good idea to get drunk on a pier."

She let the words sink in. Turns out everything she'd ever heard about Nick and Carlos was wrong. Every whispered story, every breathless aside, every snickered comment. And right there, in the middle of a gift shop carrying way too many balloons and not enough fresh air, she felt her mood lighten ever so slightly.

"Thanks, Carlos. Thanks for telling me that. You didn't have to."

"No, but I wanted to."

"I appreciate it. Look, I hate to do this, but I've gotta run. There's something I need to do."

"Sure thing. But stay in touch, okay?"

"Take care of yourself."

She walked away from him without a second glance, and once more returned to the lobby. The morning crowd had vanished, and those visitors who held jobs wouldn't arrive until after five o'clock or so. Only one or two families sat in the whole lobby at this time of day, and even they looked listless.

She arrived at her office in no time at all, and—thankfully—found it empty. No Arianna, no river of ice-blue telephone messages cascading down her desk, not even Wanda gossiping with her about something or other. She'd escaped the Monday morning crush. Or had she?

Sure enough, the minute she pulled Nick's record from under her arm and sat down, Wanda bustled in with a fistful of notes.

"Hey, you're back. These are for you. By the way, Arianna wants to talk to you."

Of course, she does. Wanda tossed the notes on the desk, where they landed with a soft thud.

"I was only gone for one morning," Rhetta complained. The pile seemed huge, even for a Monday.

"Yeah, but you know this place. By the way, where were you?"

"Nick's funeral was this morning." No need to tell her about the visit to the pharmacy department or Nick's compromised medical record.

"I'm sorry."

"Now, don't give me that look," Rhetta told her. "Let's do our jobs and get through the day."

"Sure thing, boss. First things first. Word is that the councilman's family dropped the lawsuit."

"You're kidding! Why? I thought they had an airtight case."

"Well, if you ask me . . ." That was all the invitation Wanda needed, and she quickly hiked up her skirt and sat on a corner of the desk. "It's because of the anesthesiologist."

"What do you mean?"

"Now that they've got another doctor saying nothing happened, the surgeon was fine, who's gonna argue with them?"

"But Dr. Visser took out the wrong kidney. He obviously had the films backward."

"Okay, but now you've got two docs saying drugs had nothing to do with the mistake. Exhaustion maybe, or a mix-up in the OR. But that Dr. McAllister pretty much handed Visser his career back."

"So that's what all the calls are about?"

"Shoot, yeah. Everyone expected the hospital to be crucified. Not this."

"So, what do I tell 'em?" Turns out the hospital had found the perfect character witness for Dr. Visser. No matter what a nurse like Susannah Vandermeer might say—under her breath, of course, because she didn't dare speak up—the simple math showed two doctors against one patient. A highly respected surgeon and an impartial first-year resident. Who would argue with them?

"I'd say 'no comment.' It sounds like it's a done deal."

"Maybe." Rhetta fingered the stack of messages. This one would take some thought. But not now. Now she had even more pressing issues to deal with. "Thanks for telling me that, Wanda. By the way, when does our board of directors meet?"

Wanda blinked. "Huh?"

"When does our board of directors meet?"

"Someone said they have breakfast together in the doctors' dining room on Tuesdays. Why?"

"I need to get in to see them." No matter what anyone thought, no matter what anyone else believed, and no matter what Wanda suspected.

"Well, you could always show up. How are they gonna know you weren't invited?"

That was Wanda: cut to the chase. While the rest of them wrote polite emails and minded their manners and said "please" and "thank you," Wanda had learned how to plow through the hospital's political minefield.

"I think it starts at eight," she added. "Whatever you do, be careful, okay?"

"Sure will. Say . . . can you hold my calls for a while? I've got an extra-special phone call to make."

"Okay, boss. But be careful. Those guys really *do* bite."

CHAPTER 16

Rhetta knew what she had to do. Much as she'd been telling herself it wasn't possible that Beryl would knowingly poison Nick, the proof lay in a photocopied consent-to-treat form on her desk. She wasn't supposed to have seen the form at all. It was supposed to have disappeared . . . one empty screen in a whole series of screens on Nick's EMR.

Beryl had killed her husband in a perfectly benign way. All she had to do was convince a stranger to feed him medicine that was toxic to his body and then watch the reaction. Oh, and one other thing: she had to while away the days while Nick's body slowly, painfully, torturously turned on itself.

To be honest, what Rhetta feared, what she dreaded most of all, was that she'd go to the hospital's board of directors and tell them all about Beryl, only to have them turn on *her.* Maybe they'd fire Rhetta on the spot and send her home to an empty apartment. And then what? Morning after morning spent starting her day off with a lukewarm cup of coffee and a pile of help-wanted ads?

She knew the words that recruiters used in those ads; the secret codes they employed. "Growth opportunity" meant she'd have to start at the very bottom again and "income potential" signaled a pyramid scheme, while "liking people" meant she'd spend her time making cold calls.

She could picture herself trying to study the miniscule type, only to find that most jobs paid a lot less than hers, and they had no medical benefits to speak of. And how could she even go on a job interview after that? She'd have to explain to some human resources rep that she'd left her last job after exposing a patient's death. That would stop any conversation cold. The rep might hem and haw at first, maybe cough a little, but sooner or later, she'd give Rhetta the bum's rush out the door.

Of course, she couldn't forget her grandmother, either— she'd be so disappointed. As if Rhetta had asked for this to happen. Couldn't she have prevented it, or at least had the good sense to let sleeping dogs lie? "Get along," she could almost hear her grandmother urge her. "Don't make waves." *No, we mustn't do that.*

Ever since she was a little girl, Rhetta had been coached to be a team player. Rules were rules, and all she had to do was show up, perform her job, and be thankful. Hadn't she heard that speech often enough? And if she did complain about something—like the time Arianna yelled at Wanda—her grandmother's response never varied. She'd fall silent and purse her lips; the silence between them like a physical barrier.

When she'd finally moved her grandmother into a retirement home late last year, after her grandfather had passed away, she'd always phone twice a week, Wednesday mornings and Sunday afternoons. In the beginning they'd chat about little things, like Saturday's lotto numbers, or the price of gas, or the lack of any significant rain, until she'd eventually confide that Arianna'd done something awful again. Her grandmother was polite—she never interrupted—but she never answered her, either. She would hear Rhetta out, and then deftly change the subject.

No, her grandmother would never understand; she'd never believe a wife could do what Beryl had done. And, now that it was over, her grandmother would say it was best for everyone to move on and for Rhetta to stay out of the picture.

Too late for that. She'd memorized Beryl's cell phone number, and after she lifted the receiver her fingers flew over the keypad.

"Hello?" Beryl sounded sleepy.

"Hey, it's Rhetta." Light and casual, that was key. Don't give her any indication that something was wrong. "Listen, I need to see you. I've got something for you." The line fell silent, and she knew that Beryl would stare at the telephone and wonder what in the world Rhetta could give her at a time like this.

"Something for me? You shouldn't have."

You have no idea, she wanted to tell her. "But you've been through so much, Beryl. It's the least I could do."

"Thanks, but I don't need anything. Nick had life insurance, you know. I'm gonna be fine."

Rhetta glanced out the window, to the top floor of the medical center. Nick's dark room gaped between the others, like a missing plank in an orderly fence. To her, it would always be Nick's room, no matter how much time passed. "I want to see you, though. Can you meet me for breakfast tomorrow morning? Around eight o'clock?"

"Sure. I was thinking of taking the day off anyway. Why not?"

"Good. That's good. We can meet in the doctors' dining room."

"Really? It's not exactly gourmet food."

"Oh, I'm sure. It'll be perfect. See you then." Rhetta hung up the telephone with her eyes still glued to the seventh floor. To the blackened room where Nick spent his last days, unaware of who caused his suffering.

It was the beginning of the end. Beryl would come to the doctors' dining room the next morning—Tuesday—unaware that she stood on a precipice and everything was about to come crashing down. Unaware that Rhetta would tell the board of directors exactly what she knew. The police would need to be called, of course, since it involved murder, after all.

The police. She hadn't thought about Larry, Nick's police partner, for several days now. She never did see him at the funeral, because Larry and the other officers—all in dress blues—sat at the very front of the church, while she and Eamon were forced to settle for the back row.

She'd wondered about him, of course. Wondered why Larry never bothered to visit Nick in the ICU. Didn't he make up some phony excuse about not liking hospitals? She'd never met a single person who *did* like them.

Well, with one major hurdle down—proof of Beryl's involvement in Nick's death—she might as well go for broke. She picked up the telephone again, only this time she carefully dialed the number for the police department.

After two rings, a receptionist answered and then put her on hold. She listened while a tape-recorded public service announcement urged her to consider a career in law enforcement before a familiar baritone came on the line.

" 'Sup, Rhetta?"

She could hear him clearly. Not like before, when voices boomed in the background and telephones jangled.

"Sounds good over there, Larry. Usually I can barely hear you."

"Caught me at a good time," he said. "Sure do miss my partner, though."

"Yeah, me too. How's the new guy working out?" The words caught in her throat. She really didn't want to know who'd replaced Nick.

"That's the thing, Rhetta. They sent over some chick from the Valley. And she's young, man. Doesn't even get my jokes half the time."

"Well, from what he told me, Nick didn't get your jokes,

either. I miss him, too." She rose from the desk, pulling the telephone cord with her. "Say, Larry, when I first called you, you didn't want to talk to me. What was up with that?"

"You know, it's been kinda rough over here. First Nick, then this whole thing with the overtime investigation. I guess I lost it for a while. Didn't trust no one."

She bit her tongue so he would continue.

"I feel bad about the timesheets, I really do. But what's done is done. No matter what happens, I shouldn't have shut you out like that."

"Hmmm. I hope everything turns out okay." Now the tip of her tongue smarted so she unclenched her jaw. "Didn't you say your wife works at the hospital where Nick went when he got sick? I was hoping she could give me some information."

"Yeah, she's over at the community hospital. Why?"

"Well, if she was there the night Beryl brought Nick in, maybe she could talk to me about it. You know, tell me what happened."

"Could be. That was Saturday night, right?"

"No . . . it would have been late Sunday. Apparently Nick took the medicine then. Do you know if she was working that night?"

"Give me a second, I gotta figure out my days." Nothing but silence on the other end of the line for several seconds. "Come to think of it, she missed that night. Her cat got sick. Stupid animal swallowed a dryer sheet and threw up in the bathroom."

Rhetta's shoulders sagged. "Are you sure? Positive that happened Sunday?"

"Heck, yeah. She called me up here and gave me grief for leaving the box out. Said she was gonna leave the mess for me to clean up. Not sure what's worse—the cat or the wife."

Oh, well, it was worth a shot. "Thanks, Larry. Thought I'd check it out. Say . . . there's one more thing. How come you never came to visit Nick in the hospital?"

"I told you, I don't like hospitals."

"Everyone says that. Most people get past it, though."

"Not if you're a cop. I don't know if Nick told you . . . but I took a bullet a coupla' years ago. Told myself if I ever got out of that place, I wasn't ever gonna go back in. The smell's enough to make me sick."

"Nick never told me that. I thought it was strange you didn't show up here."

"Nothin' strange about it. I gag when I think about it. Knew everyone would be better off if I stayed away. They didn't need two sick cops on their hands."

"I guess you were right." It all made sense now. Why Larry wouldn't visit Nick in the ICU. That his wife had nothing to do with it, all on account of one nauseated cat. That maybe Larry was someone she could trust, after all.

"Hey, Larry . . . are you busy tomorrow morning?" She would tell him all about her plan to corner Beryl in the doctors' dining room. About presenting the evidence to the board of directors and watching them explode. Larry would have the honor of handcuffing the person who killed his police partner, which seemed strangely fitting.

"Maybe. 'Sup?"

After explaining everything to Larry, Rhetta hung up the telephone. She felt utterly spent, and wearily laid her head on the desk.

Why couldn't things go back to the way they were? Here she'd spent so much time talking things over with Larry, yet she never really explained to Nick why she wouldn't stay with him once he'd decided to become a cop.

He'd offered her the news in a cloud of goodwill, his eyes shining, so sure she'd be happy now that he'd finally figured out what he wanted to do with his life.

How could he understand? How could Nick know that it was a policeman who stood by her grandmother when Rhetta first learned of her parents' death? That the uniformed stranger, who tried to quiet her with a lollipop, helped tip her fragile world onto its side and send it into a free fall.

She remembered a barrel-chested man in a stiff uniform, and the way a crest on his shoulder twinkled under the porch light. The memory was cloudy, but somehow in her six-year-old heart she knew that the stranger in the blue uniform was lying. She could tell by the way he pursed his lips, and Gramma always said that lies sour a person's mouth.

So she became angry, and after the stranger spoke to her, she threw herself forward and bit him right on the sparkly crest. Threads and polyester and skin so soft it squished flat filled her mouth.

The man yelped and automatically pulled a pistol from his holster, waving the barrel in front of her face like an aluminum snake. He held it there for a second—which felt like an eternity—and when he finally realized what he'd done, he returned the snake to the holster and apologized. But it was too late.

Ever since that night, she would shudder whenever she spied a blue uniform cruising by in a police car, or standing on the street, or acting on TV, even. That part wouldn't ever change, even if she lived to be a hundred years old.

Her anger about Nick's choice came to a head one lazy afternoon during their senior year in college. They'd purposely ignored the topic for weeks, and had danced around it like children playing hide-and-go-seek. They would toss words up in the air, only to take them back, or laugh them away, or quickly change the subject. When he asked her to go with him to The Shack for lunch one day, she happily agreed, hoping for a truce.

She remembered taking her sweet time when she got ready to meet him. She started by rubbing a handful of suntan lotion over her shoulders, even though sunlight never broached The Shack's plywood door. She knew Nick loved that smell . . . he'd sniffed her arm one time when he pretended to study her watch. The smell of coconut suntan lotion would drive him crazy.

Next, she rubbed on some peppermint lip balm, which made them pale and played up her suntanned cheeks. She moussed her hair for good measure, all in all, taking almost thirty minutes to look like she had just rolled in from the beach. Just the way she knew he liked her . . . sun-kissed and dewy, trailing saltwater and ocean breezes.

When she sauntered into the abyss of the bar, she found him slumped in his chair, asleep. She remembered punching him playfully on the shoulder, and asking him how he was ever going to pass his finals if he stayed up all night with his buddies.

He had startled awake then. "Hi, Rhetta. You look great," he'd said drowsily.

"Hi, yourself. You look like crap." She remembered smiling at him, though, because she was so glad to see him. Him and those droopy eyes, the cowlick on top of his head, like a rambunctious kid's, the muscles that rippled the front of his shirt.

He ordered her a beer without asking, then reached for a kelly-green ashtray that lay in the middle of the table with a shiny used bottle cap inside. He'd flicked the cap to the edge of the table and slid the ashtray closer, which he began to twirl around and around, until the green lettering spun faster and faster. She remembered it all.

"Here's to graduation," she'd said, when the waiter finally brought over her beer. Nick knew just what to order for her; the beer was straight-up and ice cold. She took a gulp and set the bottle down, before deciding to play with the bottle cap.

Maybe this wasn't the end, she remembered thinking. Maybe she and Nick would keep things going just the way they were now. Even when it wasn't so convenient. Even when other people and other responsibilities and other obligations wedged in between them. Maybe this was the start of something bigger and better. Who could tell?

At some point she remembered noticing all of the initials carved into the wooden table . . . dozens and dozens of them. So she picked up the cap and began to carve her own letter. Slowly, carefully. What else did they have to do while they sat there in the semi-dark, watching people pass by on their way to the bathroom? She knew where it all had been heading. She would finally give him some encouragement. All those times he'd walked up to her at the bookstore, offered to wait for her while she used the bathroom, or paid for her latte at Java Junction. He couldn't hide his interest in her. It was in his eyes, and the way his face lit up whenever he saw her. She'd always put him off, but pretty soon there wouldn't be any reason to tell him no. Except for that one thing called the police academy, which he hadn't mentioned in weeks, so maybe he'd forgotten all about it.

She remembered scratching a rough R into the table, only there was so much grime and wax that it didn't quite turn out the way she'd planned. When she was through it looked more like a K, but he'd get the idea.

"Talked to my mom today, Rhetta. She sounded good," he'd told her.

Then she started in on the letter D, which was easier, because the cap slid through the curve with no problem. Anyone could tell it was her initials, right there in front of them, plain as day. "What did she say?" she remembered asking, as she pushed the prong into the wood and carved out a clean plus sign.

He'd lowered his voice then. "She got a letter from my

recruiting officer. Can you believe she framed the thing?"

The bottle cap in her hand hovered over the table, she remembered. So, he hadn't been listening to her after all. He hadn't heard one thing about how she didn't want him to go to the police academy, that she would never date a cop, and why couldn't he understand that? If he loved her, if he wanted her to stick around and be part of his life, he would stop talking about the police force and start looking for something else.

So that was it. Nothing had really changed, after all. He'd just thrown down a gauntlet for her to jump over. But she was tired of worrying about him and the way he lived his life. If he wanted to drink all night and blow off his finals, if he wanted to stop washing his clothes during Hell Week, if he wanted to run off and get himself killed, that was his business.

Bit by bit, her heart was hardening. The last tremble of hope buried deep inside her chest stilled at the thought of him joining the police department. In its place, something new rose up. Not just anger, because she'd been mad at him before: all those times he ate a fast-food burrito and called it breakfast, or wore flip-flops in forty degree weather, or wasted his money on video games. That was child's play. This time, she had wanted him to hurt, too. So she jammed the bottle cap into the wood and let it take the path of least resistance. A nice, fat, lopsided O took shape after the N, which would cut through him as if she had gouged the bottle cap into his wrist, instead of onto the table.

Sure enough, he dropped his beer bottle then, and along came a stream of golden foam that washed over her handiwork. First over the R, and then over the N, where it puddled.

"I was gonna write 'no one,' " she remembered telling him. *There.* If he wanted to mess with her heart, she would pay him back. Oh, yes, she would pay him back. She couldn't ignore his decision anymore.

Someday, they might laugh about this, she remembered thinking. Someday, they might kiss and make up. But not now. They had years ahead for that. Years ahead for the anger to thaw. They were young, after all, and they had all the time in the world. At least, that's what she remembered thinking.

The memory of that bitter afternoon in The Shack faded, and Rhetta was back in her office, replacing the telephone receiver. Now that she'd asked both Beryl and Larry to join her for breakfast, there was no reason to stay at work any longer. She felt much too numb to get anything done, anyway.

She sneaked out at four o'clock, tiptoeing past Wanda's desk with her purse under her arm. Once out in the parking lot, a cool breeze brushed her cheek and the ocean called to her. Maybe a nice drive would help clear her mind.

So she maneuvered her car through the parking lot and turned right onto the boulevard. By the time it dead-ended in Ocean Avenue, the grimy storefronts gave way to a row of prewar, limestone apartment buildings.

Unlike the rest of the city, developers had spared these buildings from the wrecker's ball. They looked so elegant, if slightly bowed, with pitched roofs that made them look like Swiss chateaus or fairy-tale castles. Like anything could happen there. Unlike the plain wood beach cottages further west, or the industrial ship channel to the east, the towers looked like they hid decades of secrets, illicit affairs, and maybe even a ghost or two.

Come to think of it, in a few more minutes she would be at her grandmother's rest home. Whether she meant to drive there or not, it *had* been a week since her last phone call, notwithstanding her pledge to call twice a week, come hell or high water. Maybe it was time for a visit.

She continued to coast until she reached the pull-through drive of the Crestview Senior Living Center. At only five stories tall, the building was the smallest on the boulevard. Unlike other rest homes she'd toured, this one had pale pink walls and a tile roof painted sea-foam green, which reminded her of a Caribbean villa, the crumbling seaside mansions of Florida, or maybe a South American plantation.

Perhaps that's why she'd chosen it for her grandmother. It wasn't a typical rest home, with low ceilings and flat roofs. Here, at Crestview, plaster flaked at the concrete corners, like a grande dame showing her slip, and riotous pots of red geraniums lined the veranda.

A middle-aged man with a pencil moustache greeted her immediately after she parked her car and walked into the lobby.

"Hello, Miss Rhetta. I haven't seen you in forever!" Bert, the home's manager, was terribly flamboyant, and the residents loved him. With his polka-dot bowties and mischievous grin, he knew each resident's name and birthday. Better than that, he baked them miniature, gluten-free cakes, which he decorated with strawberries from his own garden. He was their confidant, their therapist, someone to complain to about rotten sons-in-law, ungrateful grandchildren, bum lotto numbers, or the latest outbreak of psoriasis. Bert was the closest thing many of them had to family. "Does your grandmother know you're coming?"

He was right, maybe she should have called, because her grandmother didn't like surprises and never had.

"Don't worry about it, honey," he continued. "She's in her room."

She waved at him, and then walked into the main hall, which was deserted in the sleepy lull before suppertime. The door to her grandmother's room was closed, so she knocked, and then cautiously entered.

Her grandmother sat near a window, the lights low, with a pair of lace bobbins in her lap. Lace-making was a new hobby, and she churned out doilies, bookmarks, and Christmas tree angels with abandon.

"Well, hello. This is a surprise." Her grandmother's hands fluttered over her silver hair. The shiny auburn updo was long gone, and scraggly threads unraveled over her shoulders now. Her face, browned from summer days spent gardening, looked wider, like someone had placed it in a vise that slowly compressed her forehead to her chin. She wore a checkered housedress, which she'd probably slept in, judging by the wrinkled cotton collar and the way the sleeves bunched up around her elbows.

This was the woman who had meticulously starched Rhetta's school uniforms every single morning, whether they needed it or not. Bent in concentration, her grandmother would set the iron on full steam, and then grimly work out creases behind a curtain of mist. "The school bus can wait," she would insist, while Rhetta squirmed impatiently behind her.

Much later, when Rhetta had outgrown school uniforms and preferred t-shirts and blue jeans, her grandmother would carefully soak the bleached-out jeans, and then drip-dry them in the laundry room. As a final touch, she would iron a perfect pleat down each leg, which is why it saddened Rhetta now to see her grandmother's wrinkled collar, unkempt hair, and bunched sleeves.

"I wanted to surprise you." She crossed the room and knelt by her gramma's chair. She watched the old woman's fingers tremble as she lifted a bobbin. Those fingers had once been an extension of her strong personality, so agile and bold, but now they seemed to have a life of their own. Little by little, everything about her grandmother was unraveling. "Hey, Gramma. Remember my friend, Nick Tahari?"

Names and places, dates—those things that used to pop into her grandmother's mind and tumble from her lips—now took their own sweet time. Finally, she said, "The policeman?"

"Yes. He . . . he was killed."

"Dear me." Her grandmother stilled a bobbin in mid-twirl. "Was it one of those gangs? Shar Jackson is always talking about those hoodlums." Her gramma had started to chat about the Channel 7 newscaster as if she were a personal friend. The first time it happened, Rhetta thought they were talking about a neighbor at the retirement home and *not* about someone her grandmother had seen on a television screen.

"It wasn't a gang. I know who did it."

Carefully, her grandmother feathered a straight pin between two bobbins. This was the pattern—when no words would come, her body filled the silence with gestures.

"It wasn't just anybody. It was Nick's wife."

"Good heavens. If that's the case, you must say something."

"It's not that simple."

"Why not?"

Where to begin. "Because they might not believe me. Because I'll probably lose my job. Or, what if they think I'm insane? Take your pick."

Her grandmother snorted. "You can't let that scare you. I never did. I could tell you stories, but you were just itty-bitty, so you wouldn't remember them. On second thought, it's not worth mentioning."

"No, tell me." Now Rhetta was curious, and her shoulders abruptly straightened. Her grandmother had never said much about her days as a working woman. All this time, Rhetta had assumed there wasn't much to tell.

"Well, it won't hurt anything, I guess. Remember that job I told you about? With all the fancy lawyers?"

Of course. Each afternoon her gramma would spin stories about a big law firm and its heroic lawyers so Rhetta would finally lay her head down for a nap.

"I didn't quit when you came along." She leaned forward

and carefully twirled a bobbin. "I was fired. They were mad at me because I told off a partner. I think his name was Wright. *Something* Wright. Anyway, that man fancied me, but I never told your grandfather."

Of course not. Her grandfather couldn't have known, because otherwise there would have been late-night fights between the two of them or screaming matches over breakfast, and she didn't remember any of that. No, without a doubt, her grandfather would've driven straight down to the law offices of "somebody" Wright with a loaded shotgun if he'd known.

"One time I needed typing paper," she continued. "We only got one ream, and then we had to ask the owner for more. Silly system, if you ask me. Anyway, he trapped me in the storeroom. I was so scared." She wouldn't look up as she continued to twirl the bobbin. "He probably trapped a lot of us girls in there."

"That's horrible! What happened?"

"I slapped him." Abruptly she stopped, and then glanced up. "Left a mark, too. Had to teach him the difference between right and wrong. Seems to me it's not so different from what you're facing now."

Although so many thoughts and memories had clouded her gramma's mind, she spoke as if the incident had happened only yesterday.

"But I'm not as strong as you, Gramma."

"Nonsense. You're every bit as strong as me and then some. Tell them everything you know."

"But what if they fire me?" *When* was more like it, but why worry her grandmother any more than she had to?

"Think about it, Rhetta. Sounds like that young policeman of yours wasn't afraid of anything. You shouldn't be, either."

Maybe she was right. Maybe in the end, it's what Nick would have done. And that's what seemed to matter now.

"Thanks, Gramma."

No matter what happened, she knew her grandmother was right.

After chatting some more and admiring her lacework, Rhetta left the Crestview Senior Living Center and returned home. She only had a few minutes to prepare for dinner with Eamon. She'd promised him a rain check, and this was the night she'd make good on that promise, even though she felt drained beyond measure.

Unfortunately, her apartment was a wreck, with a leftover mug on the coffee table, unopened mail on the mantel, and a week's worth of newspapers scattered about. She passed through the living room wiping a t-shirt on every flat surface, and then tossed anything that didn't belong there into a coat closet. As long as he didn't bring a jacket, she'd be fine.

Then Rhetta went into the kitchen and pulled out two sea bass fillets from the freezer to thaw. No time for chicken, and this was one of the few recipes she knew by heart. She grabbed garlic, olive oil, salt, and pepper, which she tossed into a bowl and set aside. There would be time to dress the fish once she got dressed herself, so she next went to the bedroom and flung open the closet door.

Somehow, choosing the right pair of pants seemed trivial given everything that had happened. While she wanted to look her best, she'd need to conserve her energy for more important things in the morning. So she haphazardly reached for a steel-colored pencil skirt and shoes that matched. Easy and elegant. A dash of makeup, a whisk with the hairbrush, and it was time to answer the front door.

Once again, Eamon stood on the landing, holding both hands behind his back, hiding something from her. And once again, he'd exchanged the maroon scrubs for a beautiful tan sport coat. Which made her rethink her own choices, but only for a moment, until she opened the door and felt his welcoming kiss.

He produced a bouquet of crimson roses done up with a velvet bow then.

"Thought you could use something nice after the day you've had."

"Thank you. You keep bringing me flowers. You don't have to, you know, but I'm so glad you do."

They walked through the living room, where she fought the urge to throw herself in front of the coat closet in case he decided to lose the blazer, and then they continued into the kitchen.

The smell of garlic and melting butter lingered in the air. *Perfect.* He'd never know she threw the meal together in two minutes flat, and a sprinkling of strategically placed parsley would complete the illusion.

She pulled her only other flower vase from the kitchen cabinet and set it on the counter.

"At least you have a pair of bouquets now," he said.

"Sorry I left so abruptly from the reception this morning." Her mind drifted back to the recreation hall at St. Stephens, and to the moment when Beryl admitted she knew all about Nick and his allergies. Not only knew about them, but knew they could kill him.

"You don't have to apologize, honey." He settled onto a barstool flush with the counter and watched her work. "I know it must have been hard for you. Really, if it's too much we can always go out to eat. Heck, we can even go back to the boat and I'd be happy to cook for you."

"Thanks, but you've already done so much." Water swirled through the vase, a whirlpool of liquid and light, struggling to reach the air above it. "Besides, I'm all done. We're having sea bass and white wine. Hope you like fish."

"I live on a boat, remember? I'd starve if I didn't."

"I need to tell you something, Eamon." Watching him from the corner of her eye, she paused. Earlier she had debated whether to tell him about Beryl, but now seemed the perfect time.

"Go on. What's up?"

"Remember when we were back at the reception, after the funeral?"

"Of course. Never thought there'd be so many people there."

"True." Once the vase was filled with water, she tipped it toward the stems and attempted to slide the flowers into it. Too late, she realized the opening wasn't quite wide enough, and one of the thorns caught on the vase's edge and bit into her palm. "Ouch!"

Eamon jumped up. "Are you all right?"

"I should have watched what I was doing." Together they saw a trickle of blood slide down her palm, toward her wrist. She stanched the drip by bringing the wound to her mouth.

"Here, let me." Eamon pulled her palm free and with his other hand unspooled a paper towel from the roll. After adding a few drops of water from the kitchen faucet, he sprinkled some salt from the nearby shaker onto the towel. Even though she blanched, he brought the compress to the wound and held it there.

"It only stings at the beginning," he told her. "Give it a minute and it'll stop."

"So that's what they teach you in medical school. Funny. I would have thought you only studied heart attacks and major internal injuries."

"You'd be surprised." He continued to hold the paper against her hand, his pressure gentle, but firm. "Didn't mean for my gift to attack you. I'm sorry about that."

She shook her head. "Don't be. I promise next time I'll watch what I'm doing. Where were we?"

With one hand still on hers, he slid back onto the barstool. "You were telling me about the reception."

Oh, yes. The sting had disappeared, though she enjoyed the feel of his hand against hers. Reluctantly, she moved her hand away and pulled off the paper towel. The bleeding had stopped. "By the way, you're an excellent doctor."

"You should see me in the OR."

"Well, what I wanted to tell you was about Beryl. I offered her some food at the reception, Eamon, but she wouldn't take it." She watched his face for a reaction.

"Maybe she wasn't hungry. Or she felt self-conscious with all of those people watching her. Could be she didn't want to eat in front of an audience."

"That's not it." She moved even closer to Eamon. Although he no longer held her hand in his, she still could feel the phantom presence on her skin. "She wouldn't eat the dish I brought her because it was made of fish."

"Is that right? Well, maybe she doesn't like it."

Obviously, he wasn't getting it. She brought her face even closer to his. So very close. "It was because of Nick's allergies. He couldn't have iodine."

Finally, something flickered across Eamon's face. Recognition. "You're kidding."

"Eamon, Beryl knew Nick shouldn't have iodine, but she approved the test anyway. She knew what would happen."

"Now Rhetta. Stop for a minute." Disbelief clouded his eyes. "There's no way she would have known. She couldn't have known. There must be another reason."

A loud shriek pieced the air as the oven timer sounded just then, but Rhetta ignored it. The sea bass could wait, the wine remain uncorked, the roses puddle in the sink, all while she told Eamon what she knew.

"That doesn't make sense. She would have told the radiology tech that."

"I know. That's what I'm going to tell the board of directors tomorrow. That Beryl knew exactly what would happen."

Slowly, Eamon exhaled the breath he'd been holding for the last few seconds. "You're brave, Rhetta. They won't believe you, of course. They'll want proof."

She was about to tell him she had a copy of the consent-to-treat, once scrubbed from the database but now recovered, when a second noise joined the timer. It was the trill of a beeper, which immediately crescendoed to match the noise across the room.

"Oh, crap." Eamon glanced down at his waist; the source of the second sound. "What awful timing."

With the mood shattered, Rhetta moved to the oven and finally silenced the shrill beep. Eamon did the same with the machine clipped to his waist, and then looked at her sheepishly.

"I'm sorry. There were glitches with tomorrow's surgery. The patient isn't handling her meds well, and the doctor doesn't want to operate if she can't tolerate the anesthesia. Look . . . you went to all of this trouble with the food."

"What? Oh, that. Forget about it. I hadn't really started on dinner."

The pain had returned to her palm, though, now that the compress languished on the counter. "I can tell you more tomorrow. I'll tell you everything I know."

"You do that. I want to hear all about it. Everything. Are you sure you don't mind if I go now? I feel terrible."

"No, go ahead." She tried not to sigh, but her voice was tinged with disappointment. "To be honest, I debated whether to call tonight off. I should probably get some sleep."

"I'll tell you what." Eamon rose from the stool. "Now it's my turn to ask for a rain check. I owe you." With that, he gently placed his lips against her cheek.

She could have stayed that way for hours, or days, even. "Call me later?" she murmured once he pulled away.

"Of course. I need to check on the patient and make sure we're good to go in the morning. But I'll be thinking about you."

He cupped his hand under her chin and lifted her eyes to meet his. "Miss me, okay?" He kissed her long and hard, the feel of his lips so natural against hers.

Afterward, they strolled through the kitchen and into the living room, where she reluctantly bid him good-bye at the front door.

Once Eamon left, Rhetta put the entree into the refrigerator and settled for a granola bar and a glass of milk instead. What a strange and long day it'd been. First the funeral, and then the reception afterward, and, finally, planning how to expose Beryl to the board of directors.

She had one shot to get this right. No wonder she couldn't sleep when she finally went to bed. Every time she came close, the image of Beryl walking down the aisle at Nick's funeral, a new dress on her back and a tight smile on her face, jolted Rhetta awake. Beryl walking through a reflection of the stained-glass window, passing under the Garden of Gethsemane in all of its glory. The way she sat in front of them all, pretending to grieve for Nick the way the rest of them did. Her aloofness during the reception, when she was more concerned about bumming a cigarette than with speaking to Nick's friends. It made the anger inside Rhetta harden. After that, sleep was impossible to come by.

She rose from her bed in the morning, grateful to be leaving the twisted comforter and flattened pillow, the imprint of her distress evident by the swirl of sheets. She had one chance to get this right, regardless of her exhaustion, or her nerves, or her fears for the future. Quickly, Rhetta showered, dressed, and then dashed from the apartment without so much as a swig of coffee. There wasn't time for anything else.

She barely noticed traffic crawling along on either side of her, but when she arrived at the medical center she saw a steady stream of cars that flowed into the patient parking lot. It was almost eight o'clock, and almost time for the board of directors to meet in the doctors' dining room.

So she parked and made her way up to the third floor. The dining hall looked surprisingly empty considering the traffic outside, but she knew that most surgeons already had scattered to their OR suites. For them, breakfast would be a tense, pre-occupied affair—dry toast washed down with black coffee. Anything to take their minds off a stern clock that hung at the back of the dining room, if only for a moment. For once they'd finished eating, and went down to the surgery department in their orthopedic clogs and paper skull caps, they morphed into athletes pitted against a stopwatch. Their first incisions would kick aside the starting blocks, while the second hand ticked, ticked, ticked, all the way to the last suture. It was so tense in the OR they all developed elaborate rituals to help them cope, she'd been told. Dr. Chu preferred honky-tonk music while he operated—the louder the better—while Dr. Weisenthal played easy listening tunes until the OR nurses begged him to stop.

But now, since pale pink already had cracked open the night sky, activity in the dining room was a more leisurely affair. That's when general practitioners trickled in and calmly lined up in front of the fry cook for Denver omelets and Tex-Mex burritos. Should they have a cappuccino, or a mocha today? Hold the caffeine or double up with two shots? Go for broke and add whole milk? A few GPs, satiated with chocolate and egg whites, still milled around the room.

In the middle of all this, a circular table, draped in taffeta, had been put on display for the hospital's board of directors. Chef Randolph had outdone himself this morning and had grandly placed a miniature fountain center stage, with liquid chocolate that streamed over its sides. A crystal cake plate sat next to the fountain, full of organic strawberries, Argentinean grapes, and quartered cantaloupe slices; all of which looked so inviting.

But there was no getting around what she had to do. Could anyone tell, by looking at her now, that her heart beat against her ribcage until she thought it'd explode? Was that even possible?

"Rhetta. Glad I found you."

She spun around and saw Larry standing behind her in his dark uniform.

"Whoa, now. Easy, girl. You're jumpy as a tick this morning."

"Do you blame me?"

She'd spent the better part of an hour yesterday telling Larry everything about Nick's murder. How Beryl had signed off on a test she knew would kill him. That no one questioned why a cardiac nurse would insist on handling the details: little things, like booking the scan, getting the radioactive tracer, signing the consent-to-treat.

"By the way, Larry, thanks for coming in this morning. I know you're not on duty till tonight."

"Wouldn't miss this for the world. It's the least I can do for my partner. You'll have to give me the high sign, though, when you want me to move in." Larry glanced down at his uniform. "I can't exactly stay anonymous in this get-up, so I'm gonna hang out in the kitchen while you do your thing. Before I forget, give me your cell phone."

"Why?" Rhetta asked, as she handed over the device.

"Because I'm gonna tape a wire to it. That way I can hear

everything that goes on."

"I thought you had to wear one of those around your neck."

"That's old school, Rhetta. These new babies are so sensitive you can attach 'em to a cell or a pager or a pen, even. A lot of guys drop them in their pockets."

"Got it."

Once Larry finished attaching the wire to the back of her cell with clear tape, he returned it to her. "There you go. Put that in your pocket and it'll pick up everything. It's also got a GPS so I know where you are."

Rhetta couldn't help but roll her eyes at that. "You'll be in the kitchen, Larry. That's only twenty feet away. Isn't this overkill?"

"Just do it. And give me a sign when you want me to move in."

"To be honest, I'm nervous. I've never done anything like this before."

"You can handle it. Tell the head guy—Harrington, right?— what's goin' on and show him the evidence. It's not like anybody's packin' a gun in here. Hell, I wish all my gigs were this easy." He chuckled as he moved away from her, toward the kitchen.

How she wished she could feel so calm and collected. As it was, the whoosh of blood rushing in her ears muted most everything else, including the chocolaty fountain, which bubbled noiselessly from the center of the room, as she slid the phone back into her pocket.

Finally, after what seemed like forever, Mr. Harrington swooped in, looking every bit the chairman of a board in his charcoal-gray suit coat. Striding to the buffet table, he pinched off a grape before poking his finger into the chocolate fountain. "What in blazes is that thing?" he said, more to himself than anyone else.

"It's a fountain for dipping fruit in," she said, as she sidled up to him. "Pretty tasty, actually." She would take her time, since there was no need to burst out with a belligerent accusation against Beryl. That would only cause a scene and bring on a lecture about how the hospital couldn't afford another scandal. That's exactly what had happened with Dr. Visser's case, and she wasn't about to let it happen again. No, it was better to quietly lobby for a behind-the-scenes investigation, not a full-out news conference in front of the media. Something surreptitious; something that wouldn't arouse reporters' curiosities. Nick was a cop, after all, and reporters loved to write feature stories about dead cops. Their readers gobbled that stuff up, especially if you included a picture of the recently deceased in full-dress police uniform. As reporters always told her, if someone in a story bleeds, then the story leads.

Plus, there was always a chance that Beryl could be dangerous. She had access to needles and syringes and who knew what else. There was no telling what she might do. "Can I talk to you, Mr. Harrington? Alone?" She'd also seen how board members ganged up on outsiders, and she didn't want to face that, either.

"What about?"

She led him away from the buffet table instead of answering him. Morning sun illuminated the roof of the patient care tower, and mellow light suffused the dining room.

She spoke softly, but quickly, before he could and before she completely lost her nerve. "My friend—the one in ICU? He died." She leaned forward for emphasis. "But it wasn't an accident."

"What in blazes are you talking about?"

A familiar voice boomed behind them, before she could respond. "Is this woman bothering you, John?" Turning, she saw maroon scrubs, wrinkled at the knees, and a cup of coffee held waist-high. It was Eamon. What was he doing here?

The chairman quickly regained his composure. "Good morning, Dr. McAllister. Not in surgery, I see. Well, Miss Day here was telling me about a patient."

"Do tell." Eamon winked at her. "It's a little early for that." He showed them his coffee mug, which was empty. "I'm all out of fuel. Why don't we get some more first?"

The chairman looked so relieved to see Eamon, Rhetta didn't protest when the two men wandered away together. Obviously the surgeon must have backed out from the morning's procedure. Probably after Eamon checked on the patient and found she couldn't tolerate the anesthesia, after all.

No matter what, she felt relieved to see him. He would warm Mr. Harrington up for her, soften his resistance, and then she'd try again.

Besides, she'd already spotted a pastel blur at the buffet table. It was Beryl, come to meet her, looking childlike in a high ponytail and pink tennis shoes. She seemed so happy. But how would she feel when the truth came out? Maybe then she wouldn't laugh so easily, which made her ponytail flip onto her shoulder. Her laughter, the muted trickle of liquid, the sound of serving tongs hitting a chafing dish, it all melded together in Rhetta's muffled hearing.

There were others at the buffet table now, including Eamon, who'd left the chairman's side to join a line at the coffee urn. The eggshell tablecloth played up his maroon scrubs brilliantly.

She smiled when she thought of him and how he'd help expose Beryl. Partners, that's what they'd become. He was her ally, her confidant, and he would know just what to say and how to say it, because he belonged to this group, and they trusted him.

Eamon stepped forward in line, and then laid down his mug. His hand flashed—not more than a blur of skin against cloth—

which she would've missed if she'd blinked.

Quicker than a shudder, he clutched Beryl's hand in his own.

Everyone else missed it, and they were standing only a hairsbreadth away. He had to lean against the table to do it, well under the sight line of anyone else, but there was no mistaking what she saw. He laced his fingers through hers for only a second. One furtive, fleeting movement. Not meant to be seen by anyone else, but then again, Rhetta had the perfect vantage point.

No one else noticed. Next to Beryl, the lone doctor on the board of directors chatted with his neighbor, flecked crumbs on his lapel, while Mr. Harrington studied the chocolate fountain before once again poking his thumb into it.

Beryl smirked, and Eamon withdrew his hand.

It was the beginning of the end. There would be no tearful confession, with Beryl marched away from the medical center. Beryl's clever plot to kill Nick—their clever plot—wouldn't be exposed. Somehow, Eamon would see to that.

Tears sprang to Rhetta's eyes, and she turned away, too ashamed and too embarrassed to call out for Larry. She'd been so stupid. Blindsided. She'd believed in Eamon—wholeheartedly—and what had that gotten her? She didn't know who or what to believe anymore. The image of Eamon's hand entwined with Beryl's was iced in her mind.

Everything was a lie. Eamon didn't care about her. The blissful visits on his yacht, when he tucked her in close and deigned her beautiful, were a mirage. He'd been so suave, so worldly . . . such a world-class liar.

She hung her head. Not so much to hide the tears—she didn't care about that—but because she felt weak from the sucker punch. Stumbling from the room, she caught sight of Larry, who hunkered in the kitchen doorway, his eyes ablaze with a thousand questions. She ignored him and ran for the safety of the elevator, where she punched the down button over and over and over again. The car couldn't arrive fast enough, and when it did, she lurched forward.

Soon, she would be back downstairs, at home in the executive offices. She had no idea where she'd go or what she would do then.

CHAPTER 17

During the elevator ride, Rhetta pictured Eamon's hand reaching for Beryl's—once, twice, three times—as if she were watching a movie projector playing the same frame of film over and over again.

But gradually, the film began to fade. By the time she exited the car and made her first tentative steps toward the executive corridor, something new began to stir deep within her. Anger. A smoldering anger. At first it pointed her in the direction of Mr. Tennet's office, where it grew stronger and stronger with each step.

By the time she arrived at the chief executive's suite, she knew what she had to do. She reached into her pocket and yanked out her cell phone. The wire came off easily enough, and she dropped it into the nearest trash can. There was no need to involve Larry in what she was about to do.

Next, she steeled herself for Mr. Tennet's surly assistant. Head held high, she strode past him and into the CEO's office.

"Miss Day!" the man shrieked at her. "You can't just—"

But it was too late. She'd already breached the office of the chief executive. He sat behind the rough-hewn desk, now covered with a spreadsheet that unfurled in peaks and valleys. Behind him hung a massive oil painting of a cowboy and his herd, which grazed under a hellfire sky. His office reminded her of a cowboy outpost all over again, only it was smack-dab in the middle of Southern California.

"Miss Day." The chief executive glanced up from the spreadsheet. "To what do I owe this pleasure?" He spoke languidly, as if he'd seen it all before and would probably see it all again by noon. Nothing seemed to faze him, and she liked that about him. Ask Mr. Tennet a question and he would pause, maybe puff out his cheeks, and then answer in a slow, drawn-out drawl; it wasn't hard to picture an imaginary wad of chewing tobacco lodged somewhere behind his teeth. "Join me." He waved to a chair placed directly in front of him.

Stiffly, she sat down. "Do you remember the friend I told you about? The policeman?" He remained silent, which was another thing she liked about him. Unlike others—especially certain surgeons—who fancied themselves one step short of God, he'd never interrupt someone. "He died a few days ago."

"I'm sorry."

"But that's not all. Two people knew the test he took would kill him. They knew he would die."

"Really?" Amazingly, Mr. Tennet didn't burst out laughing, which had been her biggest fear, and he didn't reach for the telephone to summon a security guard. His gaze remained calm. "You can prove this?"

"Yes, sir. They used iodine. Just enough to kill him. It's all in his EMR."

"That's a serious accusation."

For the first time, she noticed that deep creases crisscrossed the man's forehead when he spoke, and a crescent of blue-black lay under each eye, as if he hadn't slept the night before. "Are you okay, Mr. Tennet?"

He sighed and turned to study the painting behind him in lieu of answering her. "You should know something," he finally said, when he twisted back around. "I've been asked to leave the medical center. The board of directors thinks I'm too old for this job."

Too old? Mr. Tennet had been at the hospital for fifty years, for heaven's sake, but he was far too valuable to be considered old. How he could he be asked to retire? There was even a portrait of him, enshrined in a gilded frame, hanging in a place of honor in the boardroom. Taken the day they laid the brick cornerstone for the hospital, he was part of a smiling group in hard hats and lab coats with mud up around their ankles. The notation "1959" was scrawled across the left-hand corner.

Too old? The hospital was nothing back then but a patch of scrub surrounded by a chain-link fence. She'd heard the story many times: a half-dozen doctors got tired of operating in their own basements, which they had built into the foundations of their seaside mansions, so they put up the money to buy a patch of land farther inland, with no real plan other than to build a hospital and hope for the best.

With optimistic smiles and muddy shoes, they turned the first shovel of dirt, and there was Mr. Tennet, his smile the broadest of all. Under his watch, the massive iron lung evolved into a sleek hyperbaric oxygen chamber; paper charts morphed into computerized 1's and 0's; and women no longer bled to death in childbirth. He was as indispensable as the brick cornerstone they laid on that muddy day.

"You can't do that," she told him. "You can't retire." Of all the things he could have said, this shocked her to the core. "You've been here forever."

She'd meant it as a compliment, but he chuckled. "Well, I don't know about that. A lot has changed."

"Sir? What should we do?"

"I told you, Miss Day, they want me to retire. I'm not sure there's much I can do."

"That's not true!" She hadn't meant to yell. Only a little while ago, she'd thought it would be best to keep the investigation quiet, surreptitious, to stop it from appearing on the reporters' radar screens. The writers feasted on stories about dead policemen, remember? "We have to do something. Now."

"That's where you're wrong." He shook his head, sadly. "They're talking about only a few days now. Maybe two, maybe three. Can't imagine what I'm gonna do next."

Watching him, his finger methodically tracing the edge of the spreadsheet, she noticed how weathered his hands looked. As if he'd spent a lifetime splitting logs on the prairie instead of sitting behind a desk under fluorescent lights, hunched over spreadsheets and analyzing figures. She could only imagine how many sunrises he'd seen climb through his office window, and how many late nights he'd spent on the telephone. Everything was happening so fast; much too fast.

"But the murder . . ." her voice trailed off, since Mr. Tennet didn't seem to be listening to her at all.

"This job cost me three marriages," he said. "Don't really blame them, though. Who'd want to stay married to a man who gets home at midnight?"

It wasn't a question meant to be answered, and Rhetta remained silent. Even though precious minutes were slipping through her fingers while they spoke, she had the uncanny feeling that this might be one of their last conversations.

"Didn't have time for kids. Always said the employees were my children. Only now most of them are gone."

"You've done a great job, sir. A wonderful job. Why wouldn't the board let you stay a little longer?"

"I'm afraid it's impossible." He looked so sad, as if years of hectic days and sleepless nights had battered the fight right out of him. "Any hint of a scandal and I'm through. My legacy is through. How can I do that? It's all I have left."

Slowly, but surely, Rhetta began to understand. Of course, the board wouldn't listen to an outgoing chief executive, especially an elderly one like Mr. Tennet. Things like loyalty and honor and doing the right thing probably struck them as quaint, old-fashioned notions. St. James wasn't a little city hospital anymore, run by local doctors with a personal stake and a CEO who wanted to make a difference. She wanted to kick herself for being so naïve. It was all about business. A billion-dollar business with profits and losses, head counts and golden parachutes. There would be no one left on the inside to help her; that much was becoming painfully clear.

"Should I let them put my name on a plaque?" he softly asked. "Always seemed like bragging to me before. Now, though, I think I'd kinda like seeing my name on that marble wall. Show people I was here, you know."

"I think you should let them do it. You deserve it."

"Well, that's what I was hoping to hear. Now, what were we talking about? Your friend . . . a cop, right?"

"It doesn't matter." Slowly, Rhetta rose, taking a final glance at the oil painting, at the window next to it, which was warmed by the morning sun, and at the faraway look in Mr. Tennet's eyes. "Good luck to you, sir. I've learned so much from you, and I want you to know that."

"The feeling is mutual, Miss Day. You've showed me a lot, too. You've restored my faith in the next generation."

She bit her lip instead of telling him that maybe—just maybe—he'd misplaced that faith. That if they'd had this conversation a few decades ago, it would've been so much different. Instead of speaking at all, they'd be marching to the doctors' dining room and doing what needed to be done. Without a thought for the hospital's reputation, or how it would affect the doctors, or whether the CEO would be fired on the spot, instead of being allowed to gracefully retire and ride off into the sunset. That's what she wanted to tell him. Instead, she backed out of the office, so much differently from the way she'd entered.

She forced herself to take measured steps, all the way back to the PR department. If Mr. Tennet wouldn't help her—couldn't help her, really—then she'd have to find another way to punish Beryl and Eamon.

CHAPTER 18

The break room smelled of cayenne pepper and onions, something Rhetta noticed right away when she got back to the PR department. She had come straight from Mr. Tennet's office, easing through the door while he continued to study the picture of a cowboy and his herd under a hellfire sky.

Taking in the break room, she noticed how bland it all seemed compared to the chief executive's office—the smell notwithstanding. Nothing but buff ceiling tiles, eggshell linoleum, an off-white refrigerator that had to be at least twenty years old. The fridge was a relic from the laboratory—something they all tried not to think about—which had been labeled with a permanent marker inside its door. And the retro side chair? Donated by the medical records department, according to a business label stuck to its underside. Even the coffeepot, which had a singed bottom and a watermarked bowl, had been labeled by someone in accounting. None of it matched, and the bland colors matched her somber mood.

She lifted the coffeepot and swirled around the grounds, which sludged from side to side like clumps of dirt. Automatically, she put it back on the warmer.

"I hoped you'd be here." Andrew, quiet as ever, had snuck up next to her.

"Not now, Andrew. I just got some bad news about Mr. Tennet." When his eyes dimmed, she relented. "Consider yourself warned." She led him to the break room's only table, wishing more than ever for a decent cup of coffee.

"I'm sorry, but I need to talk to you about something," he said, as he sat down in one of the plastic chairs.

"Okay, so talk."

"I heard about the fiasco at the board meeting. Wanda told me. Seems Beryl Tahari has some powerful friends. But I have an idea." With that, Andrew withdrew something from behind his back that looked like a manual.

"I give," Rhetta said as she sat down. "What's that?"

"To prove that Mrs. Tahari meant to poison her husband, you'll need some hard evidence. I can help you with that."

"What does that thing have to do with it?"

He flipped open the book and held it up for her to read, but she was in no mood for guessing games.

"Can you tell me what you have in mind? I'm a little too pre-occupied to read something technical right now."

"I want to help you, Rhetta. You need to understand that."

Finally, she glanced at the book in his hand. A section titled "alkaloid drugs" had been highlighted, along with a formula next to it.

"It sounds like what you need is a confession."

Rhetta eyed him wordlessly.

"What if there was something you could give to Beryl Tahari to make sure she tells you what you need to know?" he asked. "Something that would make her more willing to talk."

"You mean some kind of truth serum? Like that sodium thing that they always give people on cop shows?" *Surely he must be joking.*

"It's called sodium thiopental, Rhetta." Finally, he lowered the book. "But that's for amateurs. Plus, it's an injectable, and I don't see you doing that without her noticing."

"So what are you talking about?"

"Something called scopolamine. Forget an injectable. I can

get it in a liquid. All you have to do is put it in her drink—coffee, tea, soda—doesn't matter. It's normally prescribed in low doses for motion sickness, but in higher doses . . . well, that's something else. It makes people a lot less inhibited."

Rhetta blinked. While drugging someone with a truth serum wasn't high on her list of ways to elicit a confession, this might actually work. And using medicine to get someone to talk had to rank miles below poisoning your own husband on the scale of right and wrong. All things considered, Andrew's idea had a certain appeal to it.

"I know we could pull this off," he said. "If you don't do something, she's gonna get away with it. You know she will."

Which was true. Six months down the road, people would stop talking about Nick Tahari. The new recruit would tape a picture, maybe a mirror—or an air freshener, even—inside the locker at the police station and erase all traces of Nick. The nurses in coronary care would stop giving his widow homemade cookies and the easy shifts. And the patient care tower would revert to its former, anonymous self. No one would ever remember that Nick Tahari—rescuer of fraternity pledges, lover of speed quarters, protector of the badlands of Southern California—had ever been a patient there. She couldn't live with that, could she? "You're right."

"So . . . we've got to get you alone with Mrs. Tahari." It sounded like such an easy proposition, the way he described it. Piece of cake, he seemed to say.

When he hunched forward, a pastel blur moved behind him, near Wanda's desk. The assistant had returned with the obligatory interoffice envelopes wedged under her arm, and the minute she spied them, she crossed over to the break room and playfully punched Andrew on the shoulder. "Hey, Andy."

"Wanda!" He pushed his chair back and gestured to the last remaining seat at the table.

"What's that thing?" Once again, the smell of stale cigarette smoke and fading perfume accompanied Wanda's arrival.

"Andrew has some crazy idea."

That was enough to get Wanda's attention, and she quickly sat down. "Count me in, whatever it is."

"Maybe you could help us," Andrew said. "Rhetta here needs to slip something into Beryl Tahari's drink so she'll confess to murdering her husband."

"Wow. Sounds like a sci-fi movie." Wanda seemed clearly intrigued, though. "Hmmm . . . I could stage a phony meeting. Tell her you're organizing some kind of special committee. She'd be more willing to say yes if I butter her up first." At this point Wanda seemed much more concerned with the method, rather than the moral, behind Andrew's plan. Challenged, even.

Rhetta glanced again at the sediment lying on the bottom of the singed coffeepot. It was barely noon, but she desperately needed some caffeine. So she rose, and when she reached the machine, pulled out a foam cup that was stacked next to it. They'd all fallen silent and the trickle of thick coffee sludging into a cup made the only sound in the room.

Finally, Andrew spoke. "It's agreed then. Wanda will get Beryl to come in for a meeting and Rhetta will slip the scopolamine into her drink."

"Sounds good," Wanda said. "I'll get diet sodas and lots of pretzels. Those will make her thirsty enough to want one."

As the two of them strategized, Rhetta replaced the carafe and returned to the table and the open-faced manual. Wordlessly, she laid her hand on the cool plastic cover, and then closed it. "I'm sorry, but we can't do this." Two pairs of eyes stared at her. "Nothing she says will hold up in a court if she's under the influence. Plus, it's a crime to drug someone. We'd be sinking to her level, and I don't want to do that."

How many times had she seen Nick stand up for what was

right, even if it meant going against a crowd to do that? So what if an entire room thought a fraternity pledge choking on his own spit was the funniest thing they'd ever seen? Nick had stepped in to save the guy when no one else cared. So what if he'd been warned time and time again to stay away from certain streets in Paramount? Someone needed his help, or so he thought. Nick would have tried to do the right thing, even if it was hard. "Nick would *not* have wanted this."

"I think you're making a big mistake." Andrew looked clearly disappointed.

"Maybe." But there had to be another way to prove that Beryl—and Eamon—knew exactly what they were doing with Nick. "I *do* need to meet with Beryl. But not alone."

"Oh, that'll work," Wanda said. "Grab a friend, waltz up to her, and ask her why she killed her husband. No problem."

"I didn't say that. But if I get her to confess in front of someone else, it will be our word against hers."

"You're asking for a miracle," Andrew said. "From what you've told me, she's not easily fooled."

True. Beryl *was* smart, and glacially cold. But what if Rhetta confronted Eamon first? Make it look as if Eamon had told her everything. Like rats that turn on each other when a ship sinks, she could pit Eamon against Beryl, and make Beryl so angry she might confess. It was worth a try. And given the choice, she'd much rather face Eamon right now than Beryl. She'd seen how calculating Beryl could be, and she didn't relish the thought of going one-on-one with her just yet.

But if her nerves held steady, she might be able to confront Eamon and ultimately get him and Beryl to implicate each other. Neither of them would see it coming, and when all was said and done, they might even shine a spotlight back on themselves for what they thought was an undetectable crime.

CHAPTER 19

She explained it all to Larry over the telephone first, once she returned to her office. Her words came out in a rush, and if she'd been speaking with anyone else, she might have worried that she sounded insane.

But Larry never interrupted her. He listened to her explain why she'd fled the cafeteria that morning in tears. How she knew Eamon and Beryl had killed Nick together, and that the only way to elicit a confession was to pit one against the other.

She needed to see Eamon . . . needed to hear him offer up a breezy explanation for why he'd clutched Beryl's hand so tenderly. Needed to watch his eyes while he casually lied to her.

Finally, she came up for air. That was all well and good, Larry told her. Except for one small detail. Something they both knew too well. She couldn't approach Eamon alone. The man had participated in Nick's murder, and that made him as culpable as Beryl and equally dangerous.

No, there was no need to risk Rhetta's life, he told her. And deep down, she knew he was right. If Nick had meant so little to Eamon that he could stand by and watch him die—even hasten the process by feeding him meaningless drugs—then obviously her life would mean nothing to him, as well.

Once again, Larry would fix her up with a wireless microphone, providing she promised not to throw this one away, he said. Turns out the local police department had enough surveillance equipment to eavesdrop on half of California if it wanted to, so getting another unit wouldn't be a problem.

They agreed to meet at the pier up north in twenty minutes. Even the chairman of the board had said something about Eamon's surgery being cancelled, so Rhetta knew she'd find Eamon relaxing on his beloved yacht, unaware that anything, much less Rhetta's attitude toward him, had changed.

Unaware that he stood only hours away from a jail cell and charges of first-degree murder.

She thought about that as she bid good-bye to Larry and hung up the telephone. How quickly things could change. While outwardly her life looked the same—she calmly retrieved her purse, doused the overheads, and shut her office door—nothing would ever be the same again.

She headed for her car, and then drove to the coast in a fog, barely registering traffic lights that morphed from green to gold in front of her, or the sound of engines revving impatiently behind her. She traveled for thirty miles or so until she reached the pier where Eamon kept his boat. Once there, she saw a nondescript sedan parked in a far space and Larry sitting behind its wheel. She drove up next to the vehicle and tossed him her cell phone through her car's open window.

"Remember, no funny stuff with this one," Larry said, once he'd finished attaching a wire to the cell phone's case. "Keep that baby in your pocket the whole time."

He tossed it back to her and she slipped it into her jacket pocket. "Promise. Wish me luck."

She didn't wait for his response, but pulled away from the space and drove toward the row of boats that lined the harbor, their masts still jutting high into the sky, looking skeletal with their cloth sails swaddled around them like that. Unlike before, when dreamy moonlight caressed the water, now a brilliant noontime sun reflected shards of light off its glistening surface.

She swung open the car door once she'd parked, and approached the boat, which lolled gently from side to side as it had done earlier.

Where to begin? She wasn't supposed to have seen anything there in the doctors' dining room. She shouldn't have noticed the way Eamon clasped Beryl's hand so tenderly, so furtively. The look in their eyes; a look that explained everything. Obviously a couple, in every sense of the word, they must have been planning Nick's murder for months. It seemed surreal to see Eamon in his everyday scrubs and Beryl in her girlish ponytail, standing together in the doctors' dining room.

Once she climbed aboard the yacht, she tugged at her jacket and made her way to the cabin door. She had no idea what would happen, but now that she was here, she couldn't turn back. She needed to see him face-to-face, to hear him admit that he and Beryl knew what they were doing all along. Eamon owed her that much, and she had every intention of collecting on the debt.

It took her eyes a moment to adjust to darkness once she entered the cabin. She felt weighty, as if she were walking underwater. Each step required so much effort, it would take her days to reach the other side of the cabin. When she did notice something—the pristine couch, the teakwood bar, the prisms on the mirrored ceiling overhead—the details stood out in high relief.

After a few more steps, she heard a noise and froze. Whatever it was, the sound had come from the bow of the boat. Carefully, she walked a bit farther and tilted her head. There it was again. Coming from the bedroom in front. Automatically she approached the door and reached for its knob, even though every fiber in her body screamed at her to stop. But she couldn't stop, much as she wanted to.

She flung open the door to the bedroom. There, she saw Beryl and Eamon, sheets twisted around them and laughter clinging to the air. What was worse? The way Eamon's arm lay protectively across Beryl's chest, or the fact that he didn't move, or even flinch? Neither of them seemed particularly shocked to see her, or disturbed enough to cover up in any way.

"Oh." Rhetta felt the doorknob against her fingers, the weight of her feet nailed to the bedroom rug, but nothing else.

Languidly, Eamon withdrew his arm. "Well, hello. Didn't expect to see you here."

She gaped at both of them, words failing her. After an eternity, the tiniest shard of guilt must have pricked Beryl's conscience, because she finally pulled the sheet up around her chest.

"Can you give us a minute?" she asked.

"Why? Do you have someplace you need to be?" Thankfully, Rhetta's voice didn't fail her, and it sounded so harsh it surprised even her. "Haven't you done enough damage?"

"Rhetta." Eamon's tone was condescending. As if she were the one lying there for all the world to see, and not him. "I can explain everything."

The walls, which had begun to close in on her, threatened to squeeze the very air out of her lungs. She forgot about the cell phone in her pocket, with a wire taped around its middle, or about Larry sitting only yards away. Forgot about everything except her empty lungs. If she didn't leave now, she surely would collapse.

So she blindly turned and stumbled back down the stairs. She wanted to run. To run as hard and as fast and as far as she could, and never look back. It was one thing to suspect Eamon and Beryl were lovers, but it was another to see them lying side-by-side. To stand in the very room where only moments before . . .

Finally, she reached the main floor. She didn't stop until the sound of someone hurtling behind her made her pause. She whirled around to see Eamon, who was flying down the steps with his hair whipping around his face.

"Rhetta. Wait." He grabbed for her.

She dodged him at the last second. Even with a device in her pocket that tethered her to the outside world, she felt very much alone. Alone in the middle of a nightmare.

"Why did you do it, Eamon? Why did you have to kill him?"

"He knew about us, Rhetta."

"But that didn't mean you had to kill him!"

"He wouldn't divorce her. He said—"

"Shut up." They both glanced toward the sound. Beryl stood behind Eamon, on the landing, wrapped in a terry-cloth bathrobe.

"It doesn't matter," Eamon said, reaching again for Rhetta's arm and grasping it. "She's not going to say anything. Are you, Rhetta?"

"I'm not?" He sounded so sure of himself. Convinced, really. As if he was used to giving orders and not taking them, even from someone like Beryl.

"No, you're not. You're going to walk away, and forget you saw us. Do yourself a favor and pretend you were never here."

"Pretend what?" His eyes, which had mesmerized her before, looked vacant now. "I know you two killed Nick. Together. You convinced him to take that test, and it destroyed him. But you knew that would happen."

"Of course we did." Beryl spoke haughtily, a streak of black eyeliner smeared across her cheek. "How stupid do you think we are? I could come up with a thousand ways to kill someone. It's not hard when you work in a hospital. For all you know, it's not the first time." She said the last bit in a stage whisper, as if she was playing to an audience.

"You are sick."

"Look . . ." Beryl began to walk toward her, careful to lift the robe an inch off the ground, like a debutante entering a ballroom. "All I had to do was find the right hospital. And to make sure, I doubled up on the dose. Why wouldn't Nick drink something that I gave him? Come on. I'm a nurse."

All this time, Eamon's hand remained glued to Rhetta's arm, but the more Beryl spoke, the tighter his grasp became.

"Ouch." Rhetta tried to pull away, but he was much too strong for her.

"But now we have a problem." Beryl seemed to be talking more to herself than to them. "You're not supposed to be here."

"I don't think she'll say anything," Eamon repeated.

Rhetta tried again to untwist from Eamon's grasp, but it was no use. *Time.* What she needed was time to stall these two. The more time they spent talking, the less time they had to hurt her. "He doesn't want you to know this, but he said he'd marry me." Rats on a sinking ship, right? The way they turned on each other. There was no honor among thieves.

"What?" Beryl turned on Eamon. "You said that?"

"He doesn't want you to know," Rhetta repeated. "He said I was the only woman for him."

"Is that so? What about our plans. You and me, remember?"

Finally, Eamon released his grip. "She's lying, baby. It was always you and me. You have to believe me."

The minute he did that, Rhetta spotted her chance. She stepped out from under him so quickly that neither he nor Beryl had time to respond. Made a dash for the cabin door, and never once looked back.

When she reached it, she saw someone already standing there in a beautiful, midnight-blue uniform. A sight that always made her flinch before, but now caused her to throw herself into the wearer's arms.

"Larry!"

He looked past her, though, to the couple by the bar, and in one swift move, pushed her to the ground while he aimed his pistol at the duo. "Stop!" he yelled at them.

Carpet rushed up to meet her, and instinctively Rhetta drew her knees to her chest. Thankful to feel the pressure of her cell phone against her side. Wrapped in a wire that had telegraphed and tape recorded every single word spoken by Beryl and Eamon.

"Got it all, Rhetta. You did good."

She felt for the wire in her pocket. Withdrew it and held it up in the dim light. So very, very thin. Like one of the tubes that had tethered Nick to a respirator. Or joined his arm to an IV pole placed beside him. So very, very thin. And exactly what she needed to prove the twisted plot to murder Nick.

CHAPTER 20

She sat in the passenger seat of the squad car, listening while Larry drove and asked her to call him the next day. She got tired of saying yes after the third time, and fell silent all the way back to her apartment. He didn't seem to notice, though, because he was still talking when Rhetta stumbled out of the squad car and made her way up the walk.

Once inside the apartment, she made a beeline for the back room and its unmade bed, where she collapsed, fully clothed, and soon fell asleep. She dreamt about Nick. Only now, it was Nick who appeared on the boat when she needed help. He was the one to handcuff Eamon to the teakwood bar, and to tackle Beryl when she wouldn't yield. He was the one who made her promise to call him over and over and over again.

She might have stayed that way forever, watching him protect her when no one else could, but then the dark hull of the imaginary yacht began to lighten and something warm and bright and unrelenting touched her cheek.

Morning sun. Streaming through the window of her bedroom and illuminating the rumpled sheet like a spotlight on a stage.

Reluctantly, she dragged her hand across her eyes and forced herself to sit up. Everything glowed in the morning light, including an alarm clock that sat next to the bed and read eight o'clock. Eighteen hours had passed. Was it only yesterday when she'd climbed aboard Eamon's boat? Saw the two of them in bed, with his arm splayed across Beryl's chest like that? How different from the way he had squeezed her own arm, while he and Beryl decided her fate. Only yesterday Beryl announced she'd doubled up on Nick's dose of iodine in a voice that didn't hold any sadness, or regret, or wistfulness at all?

Thank God for Larry. He'd been so confident; his hands steady and his gaze calm, facing them all down. So strong, despite the hysteria in the air and the way Beryl's eyes blazed. It'd taken Rhetta a while to get over that, helped along by a wine glass full of tepid Merlot that Larry had poured for her back on the boat before giving her a ride home.

Sure enough, Rhetta glanced at a telephone that also sat on the nightstand and saw the message light blinking. How many messages had Larry left by now? Somehow nothing seemed urgent at the moment, though, there in the bedroom, with soft light fading everything to gold. She'd done it. She'd proven that Nick's death wasn't accidental, and that two people had orchestrated the whole affair and fully expected to get away with it.

After a few more moments, she rolled out of bed, and shuffled toward the bathroom. *Where to begin?* She'd need to go into work at some point, and of course, she'd have to return Larry's calls. Definitely meet with him. After all, the case was in his hands now, and she'd help him any way she could. She owed Nick that much.

After quickly changing, Rhetta combed her hair and splashed a handful of water on her face. Once done, she walked to the kitchen and realized for the first time she hadn't eaten anything since the day before. No wonder a glass of Merlot had put her under; there'd been nothing in her stomach but a few chunks of pineapple she'd snagged at the board of directors' breakfast meeting. Hurriedly, she grabbed a banana that lay on the counter next to her car keys, and left the apartment.

She knew what she had to do. Even though tension had

slipped from her shoulders—helped along by eighteen hours in bed, no doubt—she couldn't let down her guard. There were still details. And no matter what happened, the moment she returned to the medical center, she'd be focused on a row of windows that ran under its roofline. To the darkened one that signaled Nick's old room, which probably housed another patient by now. Someone else might be fighting for his or her very life in that room, with his loved ones suspended between not knowing enough and knowing too much. Which was worse?

She pulled the car away from the curb, after first tossing the banana onto the front seat, and steered toward the beach boulevard. The road lay empty this late in the morning, free of workaday commuters or bicyclists with their bright pink beach cruisers, or trash trucks even. A few fast-food wrappers blew along the pavement in front of her, probably helped along by the ocean breeze. Speaking of which . . . she pushed the button to roll down her car's window to coax some fresh air into the car.

What could be better than the smell of sea salt and marine life and brine that swirled in the water next to the local pier? She saw the wooden structure through her windshield up ahead. Its wooden posts reminded her of toothpicks that speared the sand below, as if the seashore was a giant appetizer laid out by Nautilus himself.

Come to think of it, that's exactly where she wanted to be on this summer's morning. She swerved into the parking lot and spotted an empty space along the cinderblock wall. As she parked, she noticed a woman standing next to the car beside her, struggling to dislodge a beach umbrella from the trunk of a car that was much too small to hold it.

So Rhetta pulled out her keys, and then called out to the harried-looking beachgoer as she stepped from her car.

"Need any help?"

"Would you mind?" Relief flooded the woman's face.

"Not at all."

Rhetta walked over to the back of the car and grabbed one end of the umbrella while the stranger grabbed the other. Together they heaved the thing out of the trunk and set it on the asphalt. Frayed and faded, its canvas looked like it had seen much better days, but at least it was usable now.

"There you go."

"Thank you so much." The lady looked ready to hug her. At that moment a child shrieked from the back seat of the car, and Rhetta realized why the woman would bother to tote around something so ratty looking.

"No problem. Have a nice day."

She ambled away from the stranger and made her way toward the pier. She noticed again a fast-food wrapping that fluttered over the asphalt, and the way tiny funnels of sand gathered along the pavement and swirled up.

All in all, it was wonderfully deserted. Rhetta approached the statue of the seal, which still lorded over the end of the pier, of course. No matter what else happened, it would always be there. Content to stare off into the distance, no matter how many people passed it by or how many storms battered its pedestal. The tip of its nose looked pale, almost white, compared to the rest of its bronzed body, and Rhetta reached for it. She rubbed—once, twice, three times—knowing that nothing she did could change the outcome of Nick's case, but nothing could hurt it now, either.

Apparently she wasn't alone, because something moved next to her, and when she turned, she saw the stranger she'd helped out earlier. The woman's own nose was crinkled up.

"Ewww. You don't know who's touched that thing."

"That's kind of the point," Rhetta said with a smile, despite the woman's pinched face. Who knew how many people had stopped at this exact spot and reached for the metal sculpture? Something that had no more power to help them than the sand under their feet or the squawking birds overhead. How many wishes—large, small, and in between—had been whispered here, with only the wind and swirling sand and circling birds to serve as witness?

She closed her eyes tightly to block out the stranger's dismay. She pictured Larry, back on the boat, his hand steadying a .38 revolver as if it was the most natural thing in the world. Eamon lying in bed with Beryl, neither of them looking particularly concerned when Rhetta burst in on them. The way Nick lay in his own bed, back at the hospital, with machines that breathed for him and a monitor that confirmed his heartbeat.

When Rhetta opened her eyes, the images and the young mother were gone, as fleeting as the cool metal she'd just touched. While nothing she did could ever bring Nick back, nothing could hurt him now, either. She smiled all the way back to her car.

CHAPTER 21

By the time Rhetta reached the hospital, the midday sun hovered directly overhead. She drove around the visitors' section and pulled her car into the employee parking garage: first floor, cater-corner to the medical tower, last space in the row. The closer spots belonged to the midnight shift, and rightfully so.

Ever since her visit to the pier, she felt more serene. Between the smell of seaweed, the sound of surf pounding against the shore, and a breeze that ruffled her hair, she felt light-years away from the chaos. The feeling lingered while she parked her car and emerged from darkness into bright sunshine.

"Rhetta. Oh, Rhetta!"

She glanced toward a figure standing by the curb and saw army-green scrubs. The same ones worn by OR nurses. Along with a paper shower cap, which had a rust-colored tendril that peeked out from under its elasticized band. Eyes the color of uncut emeralds. It was Susannah Vandermeer, of all people. Rhetta waved back, and the nurse immediately crossed the path to join her.

"There you are. I've been waiting for you."

"Must have been a long wait. I'm usually not this late." Surprisingly, Rhetta didn't smell cigarette smoke rush to meet her, though she knew Susannah was a chain smoker, like Wanda. No, the only smell she noticed was that of exhaust fumes coming from the moving cars.

"That's okay. Everyone's talking about you. Weren't you scared yesterday?"

"Yes and no." Rhetta paused, wondering how much she should say. No telling what outrageous stories the rumor mill had churned out by now. "I think I was too mad to be scared."

"Everyone said you're the one who captured that nurse. The one up on the fourth floor."

Rhetta smiled. She could only imagine what other whispers were zigzagging around the hospital's halls. "No, it wasn't me. The police got her. My friend's partner followed me there or I'd be a goner."

"Somehow I doubt that. Listen, we've got to talk. Do you have a minute?"

A minute? She felt as if she had hours, days, weeks, now. "Absolutely."

"Great. Let's grab that bench. I think you're gonna want to sit down for this."

Rhetta followed the woman across the pavement to a concrete bench wedged between a thin ficus and pink azaleas. Beyond them, the whoosh of traffic gathered strength on the boulevard and reminded her of the pounding of the surf she'd heard not more than five minutes before.

She dusted a pale petal from the bench before settling onto it. "What's up?"

"Plenty." Susannah squinted, as if uncertain about where to begin. "First of all, I'm sorry I didn't tell you more when you came out to find me the other day. Everyone's been on my back about my attitude, and then you came along asking questions."

"Sorry about that. I didn't mean to put you on the spot."

"It's okay. But I couldn't get our conversation out of my head. Something bugged me about that surgery with Visser, beside the fact that he was climbing the walls that morning." She nodded, which caused the rust-colored curlicue to bob in place. "That morning wasn't like every other surgery."

"How do you mean?"

"Well, we have a system, right? We nurses get there first, and the surgeon waltzes in right before the procedure." She rolled her eyes to show just what she thought of *that* particular practice.

Of course. Rhetta had seen the drill herself. A few weeks back she'd been asked to write a press release about a new surgical knife; something used by brain surgeons to remove tumors in only half the time and with half the pain. Instead of writing about it blindly, she spent time in the operating room and watched a procedure from the viewing section. It looked like the nurses performed the same routine before every surgery: drape the back tables, line up the sterile field with instruments, wait for the surgeon. She could imagine that Susannah did those exact same chores in the bright light of the operating room the morning of the city councilman's procedure. Pull out the scissors, release the clamps, and withdraw the whatnots from plastic pouches while she waited for the doctor to arrive.

Susannah continued, "So Visser's already there, and he keeps looking at the anesthesiologist."

"McAllister, right?" Rhetta knew darned well who'd been in surgery that morning, but she wanted to hear Susannah say it herself.

"Yep, Dr. McAllister. They kept giving each other funny looks. Like I said, it was very strange."

At that, she reached behind her and dug something from the back pocket of her scrubs. What she pulled out looked like an enormous dime. Rivers of iridescent color swirled on it, shimmering in the light. Cautiously, she placed it in Rhetta's lap, where it lay, winking up at her.

"Okay, I give up. You made me a CD?" Why would Susannah give her a music CD, since that's exactly what it looked like.

"No, silly. It's not what you think." She reached for the disc and flipped it over in Rhetta's lap, where it landed face up. Neatly printed on its label were the cryptic initials CCTV and a date, followed by the unmistakable words *surgery suite five.*

Rhetta blinked. "I don't get it." The CD had to belong to the hospital; that much she knew, because its logo sat squarely in the center and anchored the initials around it.

"Sometimes we tape our surgeries. You know, for medical conferences. That's the thing that looks like a boom in the operating suite. Visser was so concerned about seeing straight he probably forgot it was there."

"That's incredible. But why wouldn't the anesthesiologist take the disc? McAllister must have known it was there."

"No, sometimes we use it and sometimes we don't. There are five surgery suites, remember? And it all depends on whether there's a conference coming up. First one in in the morning usually flicks the thing on. Or not. It's kind of a crapshoot, really."

"But you're so organized in there. Surely someone must have known it was on."

"You'd be surprised, Rhetta. It all looks perfect from the outside, but sometimes we don't give a damn at six-thirty in the morning."

Susannah continued, the breeze batting her curl around. "We all get so used to that camera being there it's like any other piece of equipment."

The disc seemed to grow larger as the meaning behind Susannah's words became clear. Maybe Dr. Visser should have been more worried about the black box suspended behind the operating table that morning. Maybe he had no idea it was recording his every move—before, during, and after the procedure—onto polycarbonate plastic. Maybe he attributed clicks it made to the backbeat of the stereo music. Maybe if he'd known, the disc wouldn't be lying now in Rhetta's lap.

"It's all there," Susannah crowed. "They met up before the operation in the prep area and you can see Dr. McAllister pass him something. The picture's kind of blurry, but it's all there."

The sun played tricks on the shiny disc as they spoke, rainbowing the colors back and forth. *Of course.* Eamon had dealt drugs to other medical students when his own family couldn't afford tuition for school. Why should he have stopped once he graduated? Maybe that's how he could continue to afford the yacht, the sports car, the girlfriends . . .

"It's all there," Susannah repeated. "Dr. McAllister handed the surgeon something before the rest of us got there. My guess is that it was methamphetamines. No wonder the guy was so messed up."

Clutching her newfound treasure, Rhetta bid good-bye to Susannah and made her way into the medical center. By now the morning crowd had thinned, and only a few visitors milled around the information desk, including a few salesmen dressed discreetly all in black.

One of them, no doubt a pharmaceutical rep, tried to hold open the elevator door for her when she walked past it, but she smiled away the gesture. She continued to walk toward the executive hallway. Once she stepped over the threshold and onto the Berber carpet that would lead her to the public relations office, she found herself alone with the expensive oil paintings and artfully subdued lighting.

The PR office looked just as empty. Everyone must have left for the cafeteria, or the doctors' dining room, or the Chinese restaurant up the road. Anything to get them away from the telephones and computers and conference rooms that clamored for their attention.

Which was all well and good, considering she had a very important phone call to make and no interest in chitchatting.

That's why the sight of someone sitting in her office took her by surprise. Not even sitting, really, but more like perching on a corner of the chair in mid-pounce. It was Arianna Brouchard, of all people, who was the last person she expected or wanted to see as she walked through the doorway.

"There you are." Arianna leaned forward, her back to the window and her chin thrust up.

"You startled me." Instinctively, Rhetta tightened her grip on the CD that Susannah had given her, protecting it, as it were.

"Where have you been, Rhetta? I've tried to call you more times than I can count. How often do we have to have this conversation?"

"But I didn't get any calls—"

"Whatever." Arianna clipped the word. "The point is that I have some news, and I can't give it to you unless you're here, now can I?"

Rhetta didn't bother to answer, since her boss's questions still required no answers.

"Anyway, the board was supposed to fire Mr. Tennet yesterday. Put him out to pasture, where he belongs. Honestly, that man is so old I'm surprised he can get himself dressed in the morning."

"Now, wait a minute—"

"The point is. . . ." Arianna jutted her chin out even further, daring Rhetta to interrupt her again. "They changed their minds. The cowards. They had their chance and they blew it. Which means we won't be going anywhere."

"We?" The word caught her off guard. "What do you mean, we?"

"They were going to promote me, Rhetta. Maybe not to chief executive, but at least to acting president. Can you imagine? I've had my eye on that office since the day I started here. First thing to go would be that ridiculous desk."

"What do you mean, we?" Rhetta repeated.

"You would have come along with me. Obviously. Think about it. A position like that doesn't come around every day. And now it's slipped away again. I'm so mad, I could spit."

Little by little, the words began to make sense. Mr. Tennet wasn't retiring after all. The board must have changed its mind about forcing him out. Which meant that the man who meant more to this hospital, and to her, than even she had realized, was not going anywhere.

"That's wonderful!"

"You idiot. Didn't you hear me? I said they changed their minds about firing Mr. Tennet. He's staying put."

"I know. It's the best news I've heard all day!"

"Maybe you don't understand something." The woman rose from her perch and approached Rhetta. "If I'm not getting promoted, then you're not getting promoted. Got that? How many ways do I have to spell it out for you?"

Once again, the rhetorical question. From so close up, every line stood out on Arianna's carefully made-up face. Even expensive foundation couldn't camouflage deep groves that bracketed her mouth like parentheses. Caught between shadows cast by the overhead lights and the harsh noon sun at her back, the woman looked grotesque.

"Get out."

Arianna flinched, as if Rhetta had struck her on the cheek. For once, she fell silent long enough for someone else to get a word in edgewise.

"I said, get out." Relief washed over Rhetta. So this is what it felt like to finally free the words that had been locked away for so long. To say what she'd wanted to say since the first day she'd met Arianna. To finally speak for herself with no thought for the repercussions or the future or anything but this moment. *Damn, it felt good.*

"If you're not going to leave, then I am." Rhetta whirled around and began to walk away.

"Don't you dare turn your back on me." Apparently Arianna had found her voice, but it cracked mid-sentence. "Come back here. We're not finished."

"Oh, but I am." So many memories swirled as she walked. Nick going against a rowdy crowd in a packed bathroom to save a drowning pledge. Responding to a call in one of the worst parts of Los Angeles, only to be met by a hail of gunfire. Nick trying to convince her to change her mind about the police force, but becoming a cop anyway because that's what he'd pledged to do.

"I said get back here! If you leave now, you're finished."

Turns out Nick had given her the best role model of all. If she closed her eyes now, and blocked out everything but the sound of this moment in this space, she could almost hear him laughing from somewhere far above them. And it was a big, beautiful laugh.

EPILOGUE

A cheerful blast from a delivery truck dredged Rhetta awake on a Saturday morning two months later. She thought she'd become immune to the sound, but it roused her from her sleep nonetheless.

Throwing off the covers, she yawned and stumbled into the living room, only half-awake. Last week's classified ads ebbed and flowed across the carpet, padding her steps as she walked into the kitchen. Somehow, the *Los Angeles Examiner*'s want ads managed to multiply overnight. She was supposed to spend the day reading them—with a red felt pen in one hand and a steaming cup of coffee in the other—but the papers didn't hold much appeal on such a beautiful Saturday morning. Truth be told, her vision of the future had come true after all. She'd said good-bye to her job at the hospital. And she couldn't have been happier.

Even though everyone begged her to stay at St. James, including Mr. Tennet and the board of directors, she'd politely declined. How could that work after everything that had happened? There'd be too many memories lurking there, waiting to pounce on her when she least expected it.

One day she might visit the hospital's cafeteria and notice the storage room at the very back. The place where she'd sat on an upended shipping crate and laughed along with a handsome, debonair stranger. A man so sick that he plotted to kill someone in the worst possible way. She'd have to live with that memory, and so many more.

The way Andrew had tried to warn them all that something was wrong. That doing nothing—which Beryl and Eamon wanted—meant consigning Nick to a slow, painful death. He'd tried to sound the alarm, but she'd allowed Eamon to steamroll over him when she could have stopped it. If only she'd supported Andrew from the beginning, when he first warned them about Nick's case. Who knew what might have happened?

Finally, she cringed when she remembered the way she met with Beryl on the seventh floor and actually felt sorry for her when Beryl told her about the alleged affair with another cop. She didn't stand up for Nick then, and say it couldn't possibly be true, and that always would haunt her.

No, there were far too many memories at the hospital. What if she took the elevator, blithely traveling from floor to floor, and forgot to exit before the very top? One whiff of bleached floors, plastic tubing, and overcooked vegetables and she'd be right back at Nick's bedside, holding his hand and watching him write something onto a post-it note. Waiting, hoping, praying that somehow he'd pull out of it.

If she stayed, it'd be only a matter of time before she'd have to visit the doctors' dining room. How could she bear to view the spot where Eamon took Beryl's hand in his? A quick flash, a slight blur, just enough to stop her cold. Seeing that spot again would knock the breath right out of her.

Even a trip to the fourth floor, home of the coronary care unit, would be traumatic. It was there that Beryl tended to a complete stranger with warmth and compassion, while her own husband lay dying three floors above them. How could Rhetta see the nurses' station again and not remember that?

No, too much had happened for her to stay. So she handed in her resignation and promised Mr. Tennet that she'd keep in touch. Satisfied at last that she'd done all she could to protect Nick's memory.

Now, safely back in her apartment, she debated her next move. Whether to tackle a week's worth of dishes that languished in the sink, or finally pay an electric bill that lay on the counter, or stack the newspapers into a manageable pile.

She decided to ignore it all. Instead, she returned to the bedroom and flung open the closet door. Chose the most colorful dress she could find; an electric pink one with swirls of gold, and then plucked up her keys from the nightstand. Walking through the living room, she sidestepped the fan of newsprint, and softly closed the door behind her. Wispy cirrus clouds striated the sky above, and sunshine gently warmed the crown of her head. Slipping into the car, she eased away from the curb.

Soon she was driving under the black iron arch that heralded the cemetery. Once she passed under the ornate metalwork, she entered another world altogether. *Quiet.* First and foremost, the cemetery was blissfully quiet. If a car did sound in the distance, the engine would rev for only a moment before falling silent again.

Fields of rolling green dotted with white stones and graying statues spread out as far as the eye could see. Sparrows flew overhead, bobbing and weaving on updrafts. A person, way off in the distance, knelt by a marble headstone. The sights felt familiar and comforting by now.

As she stepped from the car, her gaze drifted to the horizon. While Beryl had wanted to erase all traces of Nick by scattering his ashes far and wide, several people had jumped in to stop her. Andrew had insisted on buying a niche for Nick's remains on the cemetery's memorial wall, which rose from the back field like a granite cliffside erupting from sod.

The memorial wall faced west, of course, where the sun rose over the Pacific Ocean each morning and warmed the spot between lifeguard towers four and five.

Then Larry and the other police officers collected enough

money to purchase a brass marker for the spot. Where an artist perfectly captured Nick's strong profile by etching it into the metal. Even Mr. Tennet had insisted on helping. Since the niche and plaque were spoken for, he chose to purchase a marble bench with its own granite nameplate. Now people viewing the wall for generations to come would rise and notice a name carved onto the bench beneath them, and then wonder about who had inspired such a generous gift.

For her part, Rhetta added the most personal touch of all. She gathered a group of family and friends a few weeks after the funeral, and lured them to the cemetery under the pretense of watching workers install the bench. Everyone came, of course, and by the time all was said and done more than a hundred people converged on the hillside. They looked like a group of colorful songbirds this time, she noticed, and not like a flock of crows hovering on the marble steps of a foreboding church. So much better this time around.

After welcoming them, Rhetta spoke about Nick in a subdued voice. Which made the sound of a trumpeter somewhere in the distance all the more startling. The first notes of a jazz riff shattered the calm, followed by a smoky voice. The crowd began to cheer as a jazz trio made its way up the hill, sunlight glinting off its instruments like tiny flames.

Which was better? Seeing the surprise of the celebrants, or hearing them begin to cheer? As they watched, the trio proceeded up the hill like an undulating ribbon of silver and gold. It paused once it reached the bench—Nick's bench—and the singer proclaimed to one and all that the saints had come marching in.

In the end, she was able to give Nick the wake he'd always wanted. With a conga line, soulful jazz riffs, and a bottle of whiskey tucked away in her purse. By the time the baritone finished with an ode to Georgia on his mind, Rhetta swore that

225

another voice could be heard in the distance. One just as deep, soulful, and unforgettable. Laughing, from somewhere high above them.

ABOUT THE AUTHOR

Sandra Bretting is the author of *Unholy Lies* (October 2012, Five Star Publishing), a mystery that revolves around the killing of a beloved church worker in a small Southern town. Her short stories have appeared in *BorderSenses Literary Magazine* (published by the University of Texas at El Paso), *Farfelu Magazine,* and other literary journals.

When not writing fiction, she writes feature stories for the *Houston Chronicle* and other clients around town. A graduate of the University of Missouri School of Journalism, her work also has appeared in the *Los Angeles Times, Orange Coast Magazine,* and *Woman's Day.*

Sandra lives in Texas with her husband and two daughters. Find out more at www.sandrabretting.com.